McKay's Bees

McKay's Bees

A NOVEL

Thomas McMahon

The University of Chicago Press
Chicago and London

The University of Chicago Press, Chicago, 60637
The University of Chicago Press, Ltd., London

12 11 10 09 08 07 06 05 04 03   1 2 3 4 5

Library of Congress Cataloging-in-Publication Data

McMahon, Thomas A., 1943–
    McKay's bees : a novel / Thomas McMahon.
        p. cm. — (Phoenix fiction.)
    ISBN 0-226-56111-9 (alk. paper)
    1. Frontier and pioneer life—Fiction.   2. Bee culture—Fiction.
  3. Beekeepers—Fiction.   4. Kansas—Fiction.   I. Title.
  II. Series.

PS3563.A3188M39 2003
813′.54—dc21

                                                    2003048353

for my mother and father

Thomas McMahon (1943–1999), novelist, inventor, and professor of bio-mechanics, was born in Dayton, Ohio, and grew up in Lexington, Massachusetts. He studied physics at Cornell University before earning a doctorate from M.I.T. in 1970. He wrote his first novel, *Principles of American Nuclear Chemistry* (1971), while he was a graduate student. At Harvard, where he had a joint appointment in applied mathematics and biology, he helped to design an indoor track that reduced injuries and improved running times. McMahon's explanation of the mechanics of walking on water—achieved by a small lizard called the basilisk, or Jesus Christ lizard—made headlines, while his studies, *On Size and Life* (1983) and *Muscles, Reflexes, and Locomotion* (1984), were widely praised. In his second novel, *McKay's Bees* (1979), published two years after he was appointed to the Gordon McKay chair at Harvard, McMahon invents a colorful and exciting life story for Mr. McKay. *Loving Little Egypt* (1987), his third novel, received the same glowing reviews garnered by his earlier books and includes the same lively blend of scientific and historic detail with a gentle affection for his characters and their foibles. Both these novels inspired stage productions. *Loving Little Egypt* won the 1988 Rosenthal Award from the American Academy of Arts and Letters. Two years after McMahon's death, his daughter discovered a manuscript of an early work entitled *Ira Foxglove*; after sitting in a drawer for three decades, this novel will be published in the fall of 2003.

McKay's Bees

1

GORDON MCKAY based his plan for a new city in the West on bees because of their energy. One never finds them disappointed or confused; they have their plans and they have their hopes and they love their work. In the morning, from the moment the sun touches the hives and warms them, the bees come forward and jump into the air. They are agricultural animals, like chickens and pigs, but the difference is their energy. There is, of course, the possibility for failure in anything—nectar flowers must have the wet and the heat in some reasonable proportion or they will give up. But the bees never let themselves fall into reveries of worry and speculation on their fortune. Instead, they conduct their affairs with confidence and optimism.

McKay could feel this confidence and optimism swelling up

in his own chest. It was a buoyant feeling which often threatened to lift his feet clear of the planet. It was a feeling which made him restless and full of magnificent visions. He had an extravagant purpose now which made him get up before the sun. Each morning, he left the bed where Catherine lay in wide, disorganized postures and went into the library. In this room, where the windows extended from the floor to the ceiling, he wrote expansive letters to young men who had been with him at college. Dear Phillips, he wrote. I am emigrating to the West to become a pioneer and make a fortune larger than Copley's. My Dearest Copley, he said. You will never believe what I am about to do.

Langstroth on the Hive and the Honey-bee: A Beekeeper's Manual had been published in Philadelphia by the Reverend L. L. Langstroth in the previous year, and had fallen into McKay's hands by accident. Now he lived more within the book than with Catherine or his mother or his friends.

In May of 1855, his restlessness approached delirium. He would be awake again only a few hours after coming to bed, at his desk making drawings and plans, or reading Langstroth. Catherine could find the impression of his great bulk beside her still in the feather mattress, and she could extend her knees into it, but Gordon McKay himself was more difficult to find and intrude upon in those months before they left for the West. Often she would look for him in every building of his mother's estate without finding him, and then one of the servants would tell her that he had taken the trap to Boston on an errand.

None of this matched Catherine's expectations of marriage. She had assumed, because of McKay's wealth, because of his friends, because of his appetite, that they would live their married life in good restaurants, and move from one to the other as they became bored with the company. At luncheon and again at dinner, they would live on great drafts of style, and spill it on the floor, and never care, the way they spilled the wines of the best French houses on the floor and smiled as the waiters mopped them up.

But instead, they had come to live on his mother's estate, and life had become a good deal less brilliant. They ate with his mother in a stone kitchen, and the old woman talked through the meal. In Boston, it had been generally acknowledged by pleasant people that Catherine was doing McKay a favor by marrying him, but his mother seemed to imply the opposite. She corrected Catherine on her pronunciation of French words. She was unenthusiastic about Catherine's clothes. She repeatedly asked whether Catherine played a musical instrument, and sighed when she heard the answer.

In the first month of their marriage, McKay seemed to want to make up for his mother's lack of enthusiasm by taking his bride to bed immediately after dinner. This was made possible by the fact that the old woman had a weakness in her lungs, which forced her to retire early. On the pretext of planning to play cards, McKay would take Catherine into the parlor and wish his mother good night at the door. Then they would pass through the parlor and ascend the back stairs to the bedchamber. The moment the door was closed, McKay would allow his passion to explode open, like a fit of anger. He would rain kisses on his bride's face, and take her breasts in his hands. Often he would come to climax before he got his trousers off.

And this, too, came as a surprise to Catherine. Something she had heard, something which had been said or implied long ago by one of her school friends, had led her to believe that it would go on all night. She had not been prepared for the suddenness of a man's feelings. Is that all? This question came to her with such force that she almost asked it of McKay. Is that all? There seemed to be some mistake. It seemed inconceivable that he was finished in such a short time. The first several nights, she waited, with her eyes open, supposing that he was only taking a rest and would begin again. But he lay there on his back, with his great length and his great breadth occupying so much of the bed, and nothing more disturbing his sleep than an ocassional cough. The candle's light made a luminous forest of the hair on his abdomen.

In the morning, of course, he would be gone, and if he were not in the library, then he would have driven off to Boston to negotiate with someone about the planned journey to the West. To spare herself the company of his mother, she would linger most of the day in the bedchamber. She would read, and work with her needles, and wonder what was happening to her. She had set out to do something fairly simple in marrying McKay, but it had become complicated. He had never actually misrepresented himself during their courtship, he had only kept his mouth shut. Someone else had always been talking, one of his friends or one of hers. Their friends had agreed they were a great match. They had sat at table in fashionable restaurants, surrounded by the envious, and grinned like cats.

In the afternoon, McKay would return from Boston. If there was rain, his clothes would be wet, because he was too distracted to wear an oilskin. This happened several times. Each layer of clothing would be wet enough to wring water from, but McKay seemed not to notice. As she helped him remove his clothes, Catherine wondered whether he might be stupid. It was a possibility she had never entertained before their marriage. She wondered why none of their friends had ever cautioned her to consider it.

Among the people who came to McKay's house during this spring of his great restlessness was Catherine's twin brother, Colin Malloch, an engineer in the firm of Thompson and Gunn, Boston. He visited McKay's house in West Roxbury a total of three times, and remained as a guest for a week each time.

Colin and Catherine were fair in both hair and skin. They were identically the same height, somewhat greater than five feet, and while this did not mark Catherine as unusual among

4

women, it was an inconveniently modest height for her brother. McKay, for example, stood a full foot taller than Colin, and this fact disturbed conversation between them unless they were both seated.

Colin and Catherine had been a couple all their lives. As children, they had been great treasures to their mother and to the neighboring householders. They had been washed in the same bath, and they had slept in the same bed since birth. Not until Colin left for school at the age of seven were they separated. During the years Colin attended university, they lived together in rooms at the top of a stone building on Mount Vernon Street. Even as adults, they still regarded each other tenderly. Not long after Catherine married Gordon McKay, Colin was also called into his service.

On his third visit to West Roxbury, Colin arrived soon after ten o'clock on a cloudless Saturday. He had come that morning from Providence, where business with another client had occupied him for two days. While he worked with his pens and topographic maps at a desk with a marble top, Catherine and McKay went outdoors together. They walked out into the tall grass. She took his hand as they climbed the slope of a pale hill. There was water running everywhere, after the rain of the night before, although the sky at this moment was the most acute blue.

"On a day like this," McKay said, "even I can feel some hope for New England. The sun comes down and boils these bare rocks until they get a little green on them. The country doesn't seem so mean on a warm day. The sheep all seem to cheer up. But it's only a lie. The facts are that this is a miserable, rocky country where nothing grows. We'll be much better off in Kansas."

The gravelly track made by sheep in the thin grass led them over a ridge and then down. The Indian grass gave up a hot smell. A part of this land had burned not many years ago, so that the path puffed up a fine dust of ash when one walked over it. Conifers grew in the shelter of warm ravines, and ferns. When they reached the water, McKay took off his clothes. At a confluence of two streams, there was a pool. He waded in. His arms made languid swimming motions under the water. His head parted reflections of spruce trees and blank rocks. Catherine soon wandered away and looked for flowers, while McKay lay in the water until late afternoon.

By evening, McKay had sustained a sunburn on his back, his buttocks, and his legs. It was a serious sunburn and his skin would eventually heave up great fluid-filled blisters, but this evening he had only the blush, the heat, and the remorse people feel when their excesses begin to cause problems. He retired to a cold bath, where Catherine brought him Langstroth's book. He wiped his hands carefully with a towel before taking the book, rested its spine on the edge of the tub, and opened it.

McKay himself had never kept bees; in fact, he had only once or twice before seen a hive, and these had been the plain wooden box hives of ancient design which had to be destroyed, and the bees killed, in order to harvest the honey. Langstroth claimed to have discovered that bees will not build burr comb between the frames of a movable-comb hive when the space between the frames is kept within a critical range of dimensions. This allows the frames to be removed and the honey to be taken without damaging either combs or bees. Thus each hive may be exploited for many times its own weight of honey in a summer season, and finishes each year stronger in bees than it started. Langstroth also said that often, by the system of nucleus swarming, as many as three new, good swarms of bees could be made in one season from an original one. McKay had written calculations in the margins to show how he might expect to increase his stocks of hives and bees each year if Langstroth's promises were good. The results were so incredi-

ble that he worked over his numbers again and again to see
if he had made some mistake. He consulted Langstroth once
more, and found that he had understood him correctly. The
statements about profit and increase were clear and positive.
One could finish every year with four hives for each hive he
had at the beginning of the year. Supposing that he arrived
at the new lands in Kansas with ten hives, McKay had calcu-
lated his wealth in hives after five years in the following way:

first year	$10 \times 4 = 40$
second year	$40 \times 4 = 160$
third year	$160 \times 4 = 640$
fourth year	$640 \times 4 = 2560$
fifth year	$2560 \times 4 = 10{,}240$

In five years he would have over ten thousand hives of bees,
each of which would cheerfully produce between eighty and
one hundred pounds of honey in a year. This honey could be
put into containers and transported by river to New Orleans,
where it might be sold for export anywhere in the world. After
the first year, it would be necessary to have an increasing staff
to help with the work of dividing the hives and harvesting
the honey, and so some of the profits would go toward wages.
An isolated city based on bees would also need a wintertime
activity. McKay was at this very moment negotiating with a
group of Germans who made clocks and music boxes, and who
were therefore also capable of making hives and frames to a
high standard. They were eager to leave the Lowell factories
where they were employed. McKay had offered to provide
them houses and workshops.

The Germans were also pleased with the prospect of the
land. McKay had sent them books written by travelers who
were just then exploring the American Western country. In
the illustrations, buffalo bathed in warm rivers. The forests
were virgin hardwood. Kansas itself was watered by clouds
shaped like spires. Between the clouds, sunlight came from

7

enormous heights. It was possible to have rain and sun there at the same time.

McKay instructed Catherine to bring her brother in to him. Colin sat by the side of the tub in a straight chair for two hours that evening. While they talked, they also drank whiskey, and presently McKay felt numb enough from the cold bath and the whiskey to get out and put on his nightclothes. Both Catherine and Colin were required to help him out of the bathtub. McKay was a big man, with a tendency to be fat, even though he raged against it. Although he rode furiously, although he boxed, and even ran alone in the narrow tracks the sheep made across the hills, all his exercise didn't save him from the outrageous swings in weight which took him back and forth from a reasonably fit condition into that bloated shape which pried apart the buttons of his shirt.

Later, in bed, Catherine asked what the conversation with her brother had been about.

"I enlisted him," McKay said. "First I charmed him as vigorously as he has ever been charmed, and then I demanded that he come with us."

"Did he agree?"

"I think so, yes," McKay said. "He's considering, but I don't think he'll consider long before he comes bounding after us."

"Why did you suddenly command him to come?"

"He brought it all on himself. He says he hasn't got enough information from the maps I gave him to know whether we'll need locks on the river for year-round passage of the steamboat. Therefore we need him. If the river needs locks, we need him."

Catherine rolled onto her back. "And who did you say was going to look after him? I've got enough to do preparing meals for you without taking on someone else."

"You haven't prepared a single meal since we've been here."

"Of course I haven't, because your mother has a cook. But

we're not taking your mother's cook to Kansas, are we?"

"Come, now," McKay said. "You can't be so opposed to looking after him. You two lived together for years. He isn't any trouble. He eats like a sparrow."

No trouble at all, if you pay him no attention. And McKay paid Catherine's brother very little attention. McKay's thoughts were all with the bees, and their prospects. On some days he was so distracted that he seemed barely to notice where he was. For his part, Colin had kept himself obscure. He was like a forest animal who stays in his den, and only comes out to eat and to look at the moon. But he was as large a presence as ever for Catherine, even in his obscurity. She knew where he was without looking for him, every moment. This was the way it had always been for them. They never called for each other, because each one knew where the other was, always. When they were younger, this had been a comfortable way to live. But now it was plain to both of them, although they said nothing about it, that this should change.

"He's young and naïve," McKay said. "And he's never been farther west than Springfield. Coming with us will be good for him."

He wasn't so very young. He would be thirty this year, as Catherine would be. Someday soon he would want his share of the power that men hold over women. Catherine had known that he would want that power since they had been children together and she had seen by the evidence of his penis that he would become a man and would live in a world outside of her world. But the separation hadn't happened yet, in spite of her anticipation of it, her fear of it. They still knew each other's mind exactly. And now it seemed that their plan of growing away from each other must be put off again.

2

COLIN MALLOCH arrived in New Orleans in the second week of June. By that time, the majority of McKay's party had already been there one week. In this short space of time, McKay had accomplished a great deal. The Germans, whose boat from Boston had been late, were now finally rounded up and installed in a hotel. Fifteen swarms of bees in movable-frame hives of the Langstroth design had been located, and negotiations were under way for their purchase. And most remarkable of all, McKay had already bought a steamboat.

This was a Vicksburg packet, the *Princess*. It was long and sharp, beginning in a pointed prow that seemed barely clear of the water. There were two tall chimneys with ornate tops, and a gilded spreader bar between them. The pilothouse was a fantastic construction of glass and gingerbread, with a bench upholstered in red leather at the back of it for the benefit of persons wishing to watch the pilot at his work. The paddle boxes were gorgeous with pictures, including an American version of a Rhinemaiden above the boat's name. The white railings, the flags, and the furnace doors through which one might see the fires glaring across the water when the boat was in motion were all splendid, and the feeling of celebration and grandeur each member of McKay's party felt upon seeing the *Princess* for the first time made him feel that McKay's promises were coming through on schedule.

New Orleans itself was something of a disappointment, particularly to the Germans, who complained bitterly about it. The mud of the sidewalks was unbearable. Their hotel was shoddy, makeshift, and crowded with unsavory persons. Worst of all was the sense that everything was a race. One had to enjoy racing to survive in New Orleans. Crossing a street was so dangerous, because of racing cargo wagons, that one had to plan one's walking route not for the shortest distance but to avoid street crossings. Even eating in a restaurant was racing, since a crowd pressed from behind for one's chair. And the steamboats themselves raced. Crowds of people went to the river in the afternoon to see them start, their smokestacks heaving up the black smoke of resin and pitch. People bet on the times it would take the steamboats to reach St. Louis.

In his magnificent week of activity, McKay had also taken the opportunity of launching himself in a new commercial endeavor. Happening into a shop which sold articles made from alligator hide, he had been overcome with enthusiasm for the subtle and delicate appearance of this strange material, and had bought for Catherine and himself several pairs of shoes and a handbag. An extended conversation with the owner of the shop had put him in touch with the craftsmen who had made the articles, who in turn had led him to the alligator hunters responsible for the skins. McKay expressed interest

11

in acquiring a male and female alive, for the purpose of breeding. Not two days after a price had been agreed upon, the delivery was made. McKay gave the animals the freedom of the hurricane deck of the *Princess.* Here he experimented with feeding them different varieties of meat. For a modest cost, the deck could be strewn with beef and pork, which sold for two cents a pound in the streets. The alligator hunters could be of no help in advising on the husbandry of their animals. They explained that they hated the beasts and shot them as much for pleasure as for pay.

McKay was engaged with the task of finding a pilot and crew for the *Princess* on the day Colin arrived. Catherine met her brother's ship and guided him to the hotel where the Germans were staying. The hotel was on Commercial Street, not far from docks and freight houses jammed with millions of bales of cotton. Inside the hotel, mud from the sidewalks lay thick on the carpets and stair treads. Colin's room was on the third floor, facing the street. There was a plain bed, a wardrobe, a boot stand, and not much more.

"I see I shall have to buy a pair of great Western boots, probably with hobnails in, as soon as possible," he said. "Do they have any that go right up to the hip?"

"I feel certain they do," Catherine said, "although that would make them awkward to walk in, wouldn't it? Still, awkwardness is taken a great deal less seriously here."

Colin's two trunks were carried in and put down, reducing the floor space considerably. After the porter had left, he rearranged the trunks so that the door of the wardrobe could be opened. He transferred some of his clothes to the wardrobe, then stopped and looked out the window down to the street. Teamsters bullied heavy wagons in both directions. Even the horses pulling these wagons seemed hysterically committed to progress and speed.

Catherine put her chin on his shoulder. "You brought me a frock," she said into his ear.

"You've been rifling my belongings. What if you had found something terrible."

"But I found something nice. Go out on the balcony and let me put it on."

He sat on the balcony and smoked a cigar. The sounds from the street, the horses' hoofs turning the corner and being replaced by other horses' hoofs, made a dull rhythm.

On his last day in Boston, Colin had walked from his offices on Bowdoin Street down the long slope into the Common. There had been a heavy rain earlier in the day, but now a welcome sun played through holes in the low clouds. He entered the park and walked through the elms to the frog pond. Hare droppings were in evidence everywhere, on the paths, behind isolated rocks, in tiny ravines. The color of the sky behind the tree branches was most startling—an unnatural dark red, but bright, giving the suggestion of a fire out of control. Directly overhead, the color changed to blue.

Beside the pond, he settled among the rocks and looked at the margins of the city. There were flags flying from the windows of the Somerset Club. On Beacon Street, he could make out the individual horses' hoofbeats five hundred feet away. On more distant Tremont Street, the principal evidence of carriages passing was the flash of their glass in the low sun as they turned.

The city and its organization pleased Colin deeply. Where the organization was strongest, it became an expression of will, perhaps even intelligence. It was an intelligence of satisfactory shapes and lines and reflections, an agreeable confusion of these things. He enjoyed the way people and their clothes looked against the buildings.

And New Orleans, of course, wasn't this at all. The rough-

13

lumber shops and hotels had already taken for themselves the color of the soot which the chimneys pushed up. A new arrival could only speculate at this moment where among the warehouses, mercantile buildings, and wagon factories were the plans for a sense of style.

"Would you come in here and brush my hair?" Catherine said.

He came into the room and put his cigar in an ashtray. Catherine handed him her brush. It had a mirror on the back, framed in gold-leaf scroll. As he ran the brush through her hair, he could see the interior of the room from strange points of view and, from time to time, his own reflection.

"Do you remember how you used to do this for me? It was the only way I could get to sleep. I couldn't fall asleep unless you brushed my hair."

Catherine's hair, charged with electricity, rose to meet the brush.

"I thought McKay would be doing this for you now."

"I've asked him to," she said, "but he never gets it right. He wants to push me into bed after five strokes. You do it so sweetly and gently, and never bully me for anything at all."

During the next two days, everyone in McKay's party was preoccupied with the business of trying to find a pilot and crew. These were in short supply, and McKay would have encountered difficulty enough in signing on hands even if no prejudice had been applied against him. But everywhere they went, McKay and his party were taken for abolitionists, with the result that no one was interested in his offers. The people of New Orleans were busy and prosperous, but they were also suspicious, and as soon as McKay opened his mouth, they knew from his accent that he was from Massachusetts or some other Northern state and was determined to cause trouble. If McKay

14

was allowed to proceed far enough in his inquiry to mention Kansas, he had given all the evidence necessary to prove that he was a free-state incendiary.

McKay began by spending several days in the offices of the Pilots' Benevolent Association, where he accosted every man entering or leaving who would admit to being a Mississippi river pilot. This behavior eventually got him barred from the premises. For another day, he stood in the street in front of the offices and continued his petitions, with as little success as before. Ultimately he became convinced that he must look for a non-Association pilot, and he began asking for names and addresses in saloons. Most of these tips proved worthless, but occasionally he would get the opportunity to speak with a pilot and put forward his proposition.

Toward the middle of the week, he managed to get a pilot to agree to come and inspect the *Princess*. As the man didn't wish to be seen in McKay's company, the inspection tour was arranged for the middle of the night. The man arrived roaring drunk, and scrambled aboard despite McKay's cautions. On the hurricane deck, he surprised the alligators in coitus. The bull held the cow in a strangling grasp. Pleasure had flared their nostrils but narrowed their eyes, which glowed like sequins in the lamplight. The man departed, swearing terrible oaths. McKay was disappointed to lose his prospect, but pleased to see the signs of fecundity.

After the tenth day of searching, as he began to be aware that he had explored nearly every alternative New Orleans had to offer, McKay found a pilot who would work for him. By this time he had conceded that none but the worst would ever sign on with him, and was willing to entertain an application from anyone at all. J. E. Prigg was discovered working as a hoof-and-horns man in a hide-rendering establishment. He explained that he had been forced out of the Benevolent

Association by the personal grudge of a powerful man. He was prepared to provide a crew for the *Princess* as well as his own services.

As the *Princess* was already stocked with provisions and fuel on the day Prigg was hired, plans were made to depart that very evening. The Germans happily stormed aboard the steamboat and made themselves at home. A cage was built for the alligators so that most of the hurricane deck could be reclaimed for human use. The bees, with screens placed over the entrances to their hives, were moved aboard and secured aft on the boiler deck. The boilers were fired, and as dusk approached, lamps were lit in the halls and rooms. Just after sunset, Prigg arrived in a splendid pilot's uniform and proceeded directly to the wheelhouse. Lines were cast off, and the *Princess* backed out into the Mississippi. The night was clear and still. Her smoke rose up in broad, smooth filaments to join the general dirt in the air above the city.

Colin was on deck watching the lights of New Orleans turn away from the bow. The lights were replaced by the level prospect of the river. He was reminded, by the shapes of trees on the horizon, of a moment several years earlier.

He was standing inside a balloon. It was customary before a flight to lay the balloon out on the lawn and blow air into it with hand-cranked fans. People could then enter the bag and inspect it for leaks. At an afternoon party, he had been one of several inside. The fabric rattled over their heads, pushed by invisible swells. As seen from the interior, the shadow of a white oak made a dignified ascension of the fabric, and broadened into a fantastic leafy abstraction at the apex.

A young woman peered in at him. Her father was the owner of the balloon. They were a fashionable family, and balloons were in fashion. Although Colin was her guest at this party, he was avoiding her.

Gordon McKay happened to be passing, and he also looked

16

in. He had a woman companion on his arm—this was considerably before he met Catherine—and he held a long-stemmed crystal glass in one hand. The rush of air from the fans made McKay's cigar glow brightly. Fingers of hair detached themselves from his companion's neck. McKay seemed not to know where he was. Something about his demeanor—the fatness at his middle, the careless way he fastened his clothes, the sleepiness in his eyes—caused him to look half-witted. And yet he attracted women.

"I think it's fairly funny," Catherine said, "that everyone in that city took McKay for an abolitionist."

She had joined her brother at the railing. Bubbles of gas broke the surface of the river water. The *Princess* proceeded cautiously through these shallows. The Mississippi was more a marsh than a river here.

"Particularly," she said, "since the only reason he didn't buy a Negro last week was that he priced some and found they cost too much money."

3

In six days, the *Princess* reached Cairo, where the Ohio flows in. Since passing the last of the riverbank plantations in Louisiana and Arkansas, she had steamed through six hundred miles of virgin wilderness, with only the occasional sight of a muddy scar in the forest where some people had built a town. The river was at the end of its spring rise, and full of forest debris. Whole trees were adrift in the water. Prigg sometimes missed the sight of floating logs and ran them down. The sound was like a collision with another boat.

Colin spent much of each day on the boiler deck watching for logs. He soon developed an intuition for seeing them, black and low, among the reflecting planes. The worst logs had been in the river for weeks and were barely buoyant. Heavy with water as well as their own bulk, these were capable of goring great holes in a wooden boat. Prigg received information about the sighting of these dangers indifferently.

While the other members of McKay's party rode upon a growing exhilaration in their adventure and began to invent a party life for themselves on the covered decks and in the salons of the *Princess*, Colin Malloch felt melancholy at the sight of the Western lands. The forests themselves were beautiful, and certainly they were vast enough so that great tracts of them might be wasted while the largest part remained fair. But the work of the Westerners in their own country was miserable—the farms and plantations and industries were openly enterprises of reckless spoilage. Great wounds in the forest showed where settlers had slashed away the timber, clearing the land for farms. This had allowed the rain to erode the slopes in many places, so that the riverbanks became swamps. In this time of high water, the river was abusing the poor farms as badly as the farmers had abused the land. Whole families perched on fences and huddled in buildings on stilts, waiting for the flood to pass.

"Come up here, Sonny," Prigg called from the wheelhouse the afternoon the *Princess* left Cairo. He showed Colin how to steer the boat in the main channel of the river, then abruptly left him alone. A half hour later, he returned to the wheelhouse with a whiskey bottle and a water glass. The level in the whiskey bottle showed considerable damage.

Prigg let himself down easily onto the red leather bench. "I'm feeling kind of disgusted with myself," he said.

"You don't mean it," Colin said.

"Yes, I do. If my pappy could see me now, he'd polish my balls good. He never had no affection for nigger lovers. And what am I doing? Taking a whole boatload of them to Kansas."

Prigg left the wheelhouse and peed conspicuously over the railing of the main deck into the darkening water before returning to his bench.

19

"Do you think I love this job?" he began again. "Do you think anyone in my family would believe I took this job? They wouldn't. They wouldn't believe it. My brothers and my pappy and me were slave hunters. We hunted them and caught them everywhere. I'm no nigger lover. I wish I had never heard of you people. I shouldn't be doing this. I should be back there in New Orleans cutting the feet off dead cows."

When Colin reported the substance of this conversation to McKay later in the evening, McKay did not seem alarmed.

"There is already a class of Americans," McKay said, "who are bitter and remorseful because they are too awkward to make themselves rich in a rich land. These are the sons and daughters of peasants who have giant appetites but no talents. When their parents were serfs in Europe, they could delude themselves into thinking that freedom would solve their problems, but here they are free and too stupid to know what to do about it. Prigg is one of these people. He'd like to own the *Princess,* he'd like to own the hide-rendering plant where we found him, but he never shall, even though the ambition is strong in him. But he'll do enough work to get by, and that should be sufficient for us. He knows the river, and can navigate in it even in his confused state of mind."

Well after midnight, Colin was awakened by the shouts of children. He sat up in his bunk and drew aside the curtains at the porthole. The boat was motionless—she might have been tied up at a dock. Perhaps she was aground. The children had been shouting outside Colin's porthole but were now somewhere else. He heard the footsteps of a child running by, but never saw him.

Now there was quiet again, and the sense of emergency disappeared. Colin relaxed, almost into sleep.

"Wake up, you people on that boat!" a voice said. "Your boat is burning!"

This was true. The fire had been set in a pile of newspapers and deck chairs wet with lamp oil on the forward boiler deck. Before Colin could reach it, the flames were ten feet high, and the fire had nearly consumed the base of the flagpole. The eyes of half a dozen children of various ages glittered from the riverbank, which was now directly below the white deck railings. Colin threw the children a bucket. They filled it with Mississippi mud and passed it back. The mud attached itself to the burning wood the way an insect attaches its house to a stick. The first bucketful cut the flames in half, and the third put the fire out. By the time McKay, Catherine, and the Germans had arrived, there was nothing left of the fire but a smoking pyramid of river bottom.

"Which one of you little vagrants set this fire?" McKay said to the children.

Colin was astonished. How was it possible that McKay could be so ignorant of the forces which threatened him?

"I don't suppose any one of them set it," Colin said. "There they are, standing down there in the mud, and the fire was up here on the deck. These children couldn't have harmed us from where they stand. On the other hand, the pilot and crew are no longer aboard this boat."

McKay scanned the heads of the people collected around him. He looked up to the wheelhouse, which was now empty and dark. Steam whistling from the escape pipes condensed into two plumes, which glowed white in the severe moonlight and then evaporated. The *Princess's* chimneys were closer than they should have been to a tree branch. She had water at her stern but was otherwise imprisoned by the land.

"If what you say is true," McKay said slowly, "I shall see that he is tracked down, and both his kidneys roasted over an open fire. This way of treating people is too outrageous, even in the West."

Colin arranged for the services of two of the oldest children to be enlisted in rescuing the *Princess* from the mud flats. These were the brothers Edward and Jiffy Appleton, whose parents were tenant farmers nearby. By morning, Edward and Jiffy had spread a general enthusiasm along the riverbank for helping the steamboat off the shoal, and a great many men, mules, and oxen were hired for the purpose. Blocks and tackle were removed from the *Princess's* cranes and run to stout trees on the banks at her stern. The passengers, alligators, bees, and everything else that represented movable weight were transferred to the riverbank.

Edward and Jiffy's mother turned out to be a handsome woman of forty-five who never wore shoes but sometimes chewed tobacco.

"I was brought up on a plantation fourteen miles south of here where the river takes a sharp bend," she told Colin, "and we always had steamboats coming into our chicken yard. In the spring rise, our front lawn would flood, and the steamboat pilots would think there was a chute between my mother's porch and the hog-killing tree. We'd look out the window, and here would be this steamboat coming as fast as you can believe toward the house. My daddy kept a special team of oxen for nothing else but putting steamboats back in the water. Once, a great big one come up as far as my mother's root garden, and they never did get it to go back. Some men came with saws and axes and chopped it all apart."

Before evening, the *Princess* was back in the Mississippi again, and did not appear to be leaking too badly to proceed. Colin inspected the inside of the hull and concluded that there was no threatening damage. With the help of one of the Germans, he brought up a head of steam and determined that the engine and paddle wheels were serviceable. As Edward and Jiffy knew the river between that point and St. Louis, McKay proposed to hire them as guides. Although the boys looked younger, possibly because of poor diet, they were in fact sixteen and seventeen. The boys themselves were enthusiastic, but their mother wept when she heard they were to go.

"It seemed we had all the time in the world," she said, "to get prosperous enought to give the children what they needed. When we got married, we had nothing, and the babies came soon. We were miserable sometimes, but we weren't afraid. The children would never want for anything, because we were going to get it for them next year. We always said we were going to live in a house that stays dry all the year and eat chocolate after every meal. Now they're leaving, and we'll never give them what we promised. The younger children will still be here, and so perhaps we'll do better by them, but I can't believe Edward and Jiffy are leaving home. We were always sure there was so much time left."

4

COLIN now assumed responsibility for piloting the *Princess* through to St. Louis. From the moment he began, he found nothing really strange about steering the boat and controlling her speed. He found all his surprises and difficulties in the river bed. One simply could not anticipate where the deep channel would be. In bends, the deep water might be at the convex lip, where an abrupt change in color showed the point of mixing of the relatively clear surface water and the stagnant water of the bank. Just as often, one might encounter an invisible bar in the same place a channel had been found another time. Edward helped a German man fire the boiler while Jiffy stood beside the wheel and pointed out dangers in the river. In the broad places, Jiffy sang and played a mouth organ. He also blew the steam whistle a great deal. Every passing boat or raft received a deafening salute, as did the sight of each river town. When Jiffy recognized someone he knew on a raft or walking along the bank, he first sent up an outrageous volley of whistle blasts and then displayed himself on the main deck.

These high spirits infected Colin as well. There was some quality of the bright sky, now utterly without clouds, which made one pleased with the prospect of things to come.

But in the pleasure was a sense of urgency. In such beautiful circumstances, on the planes of a warm river flowing out of some distant heart, he was blocked from entering the landscape. And yet he must go into it! The Westerners already here were cutting, plowing, hoeing, planting, hammering, and otherwise taking the land for their own purposes. From the forest, the sounds of saws and axes flooded out in steady waves. The sounds gave him a giddy feeling. What were people doing in the woods? They were seizing the land, and they were doing it hastily. And yet, this was what he himself must do! He must go into the forest and take a piece of this beautiful land for himself. This was his instinct, and he could not get free of it, no matter how ugly and contemptible he found the works of others who had responded to this same instinct.

"I'd like to know what goes on in a man's mind," Catherine said when she joined him just before noon. "I have a very practical interest."

"Your interest may be practical," he said, "but your question isn't. Which man's mind do you want to know? We're very diverse."

"I'll take an answer from you," she said, "and I'll assume it works for somebody else."

"That doesn't sound like a good idea. I don't think like McKay at all."

"I'm not talking about thinking. I'm talking about feeling."

"I don't do that like McKay, either."

"No?" Catherine lay back on the bench and closed her eyes.

The sun gave her face a bright and a dark side. Her hair reflected the light. It lay curved over her shoulders like a spoon. "You're acting angry," she said. "Don't."

And then she flew up and kissed him on the mouth. "I still love you!" she said. She clung to him. They were so much alike! Their eyes were the same, and their sharp noses and chins. They were alike in their faces, in their taste in food, and in their determination to have what they had set their hearts upon. They were twins in everything except their sex, but even in this they were reflections of each other.

"You mustn't think McKay is taking away your love! I'll always love you best!"

"I think he's ridiculous," Colin said.

"Of course he's ridiculous," Catherine told him. "He's a perfectly ridiculous person. But if we spent our time avoiding ridiculous people, we'd always be crossing to the other side of the street." She held Colin fast. His skin was warm where she pressed it. "Besides," she said, "he likes you very much. He's told me so himself. He respects your judgment. You're so practical."

"And he's so rich."

"He isn't, really. It's his ambition that makes him appear rich."

Colin would cheerfully admit that McKay was ambitious. He had known McKay slightly before Catherine had married him when, like many of his social peers, McKay had been a land speculator. None of his proposed routes for railroads in Massachusetts and New Hampshire had come to anything more than the bullying of farmers for their land. This bullying was considered something of a sport. Exaggerated stories were told about it later at the Somerset Club.

But whereas McKay's friends made substantial profits, and reinvested their profits again and again until they built fortunes, McKay himself fell behind at the game. It became known

26

that he had little sense. He wasted money famously. He bought wetlands near the ocean under the impression they could be drained and converted to pasture. He fell victim to a fraudulent scheme to bring a symphony orchestra to Boston. He spent large sums on the entertainment of women.

Worse was the lack of any evidence of conscious knowledge on his part of what he was trying to do. He seemed particularly ignorant of what he was doing to other people. This last thought worried Colin the most.

In St. Louis, McKay hired a new pilot, a Massachusetts man called William Sewall who made a speciality of taking Free Staters to Kansas. He was a tall, gaunt man who had reached that age and disposition which causes some men to consider political office and others to throw away the affections of their wives. This sense of obligation to worlds broader than the ones of their younger lives drives some men to greatness, but for most it ends in compromise. The voyages of discovery are taken as part of an organized tour, or they are forgotten altogether.

Not so in the case of Mr. William Sewall. He and his brother were the owners of a successful textile mill in the town of Fitchburg, but in their middle years they had abandoned this family enterprise to become ice barons. They had procured one of Nathaniel Wyeth's horse-drawn ice-cutting machines and set it to work harvesting ice from a local pond. They had taken their first crop to Havana, where other New England men had already created a demand for ice to be used in cooling drinks and making ice cream. There they built an icehouse of their own design, from which they personally sold ice in small quantities at fancy prices. Rich Cubans spent fortunes on ice, and for some of them it became an addiction.

But with the arrival of yellow fever in Havana, the Sewalls were ruined. They were ruined because it was discovered that the fever could be broken by applying ice to the forehead of the afflicted person. The Sewalls' product, which they had brought for trivial entertainment, now had the power to bring people back from death. What had been an expensive luxury now became a priceless medicine, and the Sewalls knew that they must now make their ice available to Havana's poor and sick without cost. They delivered blocks to hospitals and churches, and explained how the ice was to be preserved and used.

In the course of this ministry, William Sewall met a young Catholic woman of color and fell in love with her. Her neck was long and slender, as if the most subtle reptilian gene had sometime flowed into her African ancestry. Her legs were as thin as those of some range animal, but her back was strong enough to carry the ice Sewall cut out for her in sixty-pound blocks. They delivered the ice not only throughout Havana but in the countryside, where the young woman was known in every village. They spoke together only in French, her native language. They lived as man and wife. In a remote village in the mountains, they began construction of an infirmary.

The stores of ice were exhausted by the time Sewall's young woman herself contracted the fever. She burned up in his arms. She went into sleep and then into death as hastily as if actual flames were taking her.

With the end of the ice, the Sewalls left Cuba. While his brother went home to Massachusetts, to the textile mill and the debts their adventure had left them, William sailed to New Orleans. There he heard of the profits to be made taking free state settlers into the new Kansas lands. Using the last of his ice capital for tuition, he obtained a river pilot's license for the upper Mississippi and the Kansas, and was now more prosperous than he had ever been in his life.

Sewall admired the lines and the construction of the *Princess* and seemed pleased with the prospect of her command.

"How awful," Catherine said, after a day of running in the clear water north of St. Louis. "Our new pilot seems to be sillier than Prigg. He's stopped the engine, and now he's chasing a bird all over the top deck."

"What kind of bird?" McKay asked.

"How should I know what kind of bird? I don't know birds."

"I'll have a look," McKay said.

He climbed the stairs to the hurricane deck, but at the top, Sewall motioned for him to be silent and stay where he was. He was threading a string over the roof beams. The string led to the apex of a net made of a fine material suspended above the deck. Directly beneath the net, Sewall had scattered a variety of seeds.

The object of the trap was a small undistinguished bird. It was perched on the railing of the hurricane deck, motionless. Behind it, the brown color of the Mississippi turned slowly. The *Princess* was dead in the water, spinning with the great eddies, and all because of a bird which weighed less than a five-cent piece. The bird made up its mind to have the seeds, changed its mind, then changed it back again. It flew down to the deck. This seed, that one, which one was best? It hopped from place to place, but never under the net. It picked up the seeds in absolutely invisible jerks.

And then it made its mistake; it hopped under the net. Sewall let go of the string and caught it.

"Got ya," he said.

"What is it?" McKay asked. "It looks like some kind of barn twit."

"Nonsense," said Sewall. "It's a finch. See that he doesn't get away while I fetch his cage."

He almost collided with Catherine at the head of the stairs. "Pardon me," he said as he flew by.

"What are you doing up here?" Catherine wanted to know.

"I'm watching this bird in this net," McKay said.

29

"There's no one driving the boat."

"I know."

Aren't you afraid we'll run into something?"

"I'm trying *not* to be afraid. It's better to be *calm* when things are out of control," McKay said.

Sewall returned with a small wicker bird cage. He removed the bottom, shook the bird into it, then closed it up. "Come up to the wheelhouse and have a cup of tea," he said. They followed him up the stairs.

Sewall had made the wheelhouse very much his own. Books, maps, animal cages, and wooden boxes were piled in the corners. Butterflies and wasps under glass hung on the walls. Plant specimens pressed between sheets of glass were on the floor. Sewall lit a wood stove and set a kettle on it.

"What's all this?" Catherine said.

"This is the clutter of a naturalist," Sewall told her, "which is what I am."

"You caught all these things?"

"I caught them or picked them, depending on whether they were animals or plants."

"How fascinating."

"Yes," Sewall said, spooning the tea into the teapot. "I suppose it is fascinating. I originally took this up for money, but now I find I'm interested in plants and animals for their own sweet selves."

"You do this for money?"

"Yes, indeed," he said. "Everything you see here will be on its way to New Haven or Cambridge or London after I've studied it enough to be sure that it represents a valuable specimen."

"Why?" Catherine asked him. "I mean, why would anyone pay you for a butterfly? They're certainly pretty, but there are so many of them, and they're everywhere. I don't see why anybody who wanted one couldn't simply go out and get one for himself."

Sewall opened a trunk and took out three cups and saucers. "Museums of natural history don't want just one butterfly," he said. "They want them all. That is, they want one of all the species."

"And how many species are there?"

"No one knows," he said. "And no one knows why there are so many or how they came into being. They might have all been created in a moment, but if that's how it happened, then were they created as adults, or as children, or as seeds? If you were to hit your head on a door and lose your memory, and later asked me what your whole life had been before, I might say that you had always been as you are now. Perhaps you would believe me for a while, but sooner or later you would see that plants and animals grow, and you would wonder how your own history could be permanent if theirs was so changeable. You would wonder why some live and others die.

"In the Caribbean, the number and diversity of species is overwhelming. Everywhere you look, something is moving. It is impossible to imagine the land nude, without its plants and animals, but it's a plain fact that without continuous reproduction the most beautiful tropical island would become a desert. In all the obvious diversity among species, there is only one diversity which really matters, and that is the difference between the sexes, because it makes this fertile reproduction possible.

"It seems to me that the lives of species are like the lives of individuals. They are conceived by accident, they live through a precarious infancy, they trade blows with the world all around them, and either live or die on the outcome. I am convinced that species are not immutable. The ones I collect today are not the same ones my descendants could find thou-

31

sands of years in the future. Between now and then, an uncountable number of courtships and copulations will take place, and from all the crosses and hybrids some will be fertile and others will be sterile, some will be prosperous and others will fail.

"Most of the people I take to Kansas don't care about natural history. If you ask me, this is a mistake, because it won't be long before the living things already in the Western lands will make the people I take there rich or kill them off. I might like to live in splendid isolation myself, if I thought there was such a thing. But there isn't, not unless you count the kind of isolation that only goes on in people's minds."

5

GORDON MCKAY felt restlessness growing up again inside him, and was troubled by it. The restlessness took over his feelings and made them keener than they should have been. In his first three weeks in the Western lands he had put the *Princess,* the alligators, the bees, the Germans, and Colin and Catherine all together and launched them out into the Mississippi River. This was real progress! He was elated! They moved toward Kansas with absolute certainty. There was no possibility that they would become lost, since the river flowed from Kansas, and the *Princess* floated on the river. Even Prigg's treachery had been satisfactory in some magical way, because he hadn't been able to harm them, or even delay them seriously.

But now, with this danger quite safely in the past, McKay felt frightened. The feeling came over him and settled in his bowels like influenza. It caused his hands to jerk when he didn't expect them to, and it caused his spine to stiffen. He wanted to run and jump, but this was impossible, or at least undignified, on a steamboat. In his bed, before sleep, the cabin seemed to lurch suddenly, and he felt the boat caught in a terrible vortex. The force of the vortex threatened to throw him against the wall, and how could any force so strong be imaginary? Yet Catherine felt it not at all, and slept beside him peacefully.

McKay let his anxiety come to rest on the bees. Langstroth said they could be moved, even great distances, as long as their needs were provided for. There must be adequate stores of honey and pollen. They must have water. The hives must be ventilated properly. They must not be left in the direct sun, where the heat could exhaust the bees and melt the combs.

McKay spent hours beside the hives each day. He listened to the sounds the bees made. Their sound was always the same, a low growl of confidence and wildness. He put his ear to the warm wood. He could hear their wings, but never their footsteps. Their wings beat a draft among the combs, a draft which smelled powerfully of honey when it emerged. He reclined on the deck and read Langstroth's book. In the afternoon, shadows from the boughs of giant cedar and cottonwood trees shaded the pages as the *Princess* passed under them.

In Kansas City, McKay decided that the bees should be allowed to fly for a day in order to cleanse themselves. They would not excrete their feces in the hive, and therefore risked death if they were not allowed to fly out and relieve themselves in the open air. The *Princess* tied up at the end of a row of commercial wharfs. The smell of cattle and stockyards was strong here. McKay put on his bee veil and gloves. When he removed the screens from the hive entrances, the bees streamed out in black jets.

"You let them get away," Catherine said. "Why did you do that?"

34

"It says in the book they'll come back," he told her.

The Germans were tired of river travel and wanted to see what there was in Kansas City. It was agreed that Sewall would stay with the boat, but the rest of the party would make an expedition into the town. By this time the bees had found some tupelos nearby and were occupied with carrying nectar to the hives.

After only an hour's inspection, the Germans agreed that New Orleans was Vienna compared to this place. Cattle were driven down the main streets to the slaughterhouses, so that the streets were paved with a paste of mud and animal dung. The air smelled of tallow and burning hair. The sounds of hammers rang out everywhere, and saws: Kansas City would be twice the size next year. Great piles of raw lumber here and there showed how enthusiastic everyone was about the growth of their town. As in New Orleans and St. Louis, there were many saloons but few restaurants. They took their lunch in a "refreshment parlor" in the company of what seemed like the entire population of the town.

"We've seen this so often, now, that I suppose we must admit that these are the ways of our new adopted country," Mrs. Finger told McKay. Mrs. Finger was the widow of a craftsman who made the elegant brass clockwork of music boxes. Her husband had once made an articulated duck which would walk to the edge of a pond under its own power, jump in, and swim around playing Mozart for a quarter of an hour on a single winding. "I've been making an effort to enjoy eating a meal in fifteen minutes," she said. "There's a nice sense of democracy about it. Each person is served the same as his neighbor. Everyone gets one knife and one fork to last through the whole meal. We start together, eat as fast as we can, and finish together. If you linger over your food, you can expect a good-natured poke in the ribs from someone who is waiting for your chair. Everyone laughs with his mouth full of egg or custard

35

and asks you where you are from. Simplicity and equality are things I thought I would like about America, but now that I'm in the midst of them, I find they're not all they were cracked up to be."

In the afternoon, McKay led Colin and Catherine to a hardware store, where he bought a spade. He then hired a surrey and drove several miles out into the country. He stopped in a totally undistinguished place on a grassy rise slightly higher than the river valley and its flood plain, which were just visible through the cottonwoods. The new spade flashed like a weapon in his hand as he marched twenty yards into the field and began to dig.

The black dirt flew up in little geysers as McKay pried at the soil. Once he was through the turf, the digging went more easily. He thrust the shovel in and pulled it out, and never broke his rhythm. The earth accumulated in a pile which finally grew to be a small hill. He didn't stop until the hole was as deep as the spade handle was long.

"Look at that," he said. "I've only just now struck clay. The topsoil is close to five feet thick here. This land can be plowed and farmed for centuries without wearing it out. You're looking at the greatest fortune ever discovered."

As he said this, he swept his hand across the horizon. Country houses, hedges, flower gardens, cathedrals, fruit trees, farm animals, stone stiles—all these were possibilities for a cultivated future, but now there was only a grassy plain broken by solitary cottonwood trees.

"There can be no doubt that people will come here and build farms on this land, and these farms will be rich enough to feed the earth's population. There will be cities, too. Perhaps that miserable enterprise in the valley will become grander than London. There are pieces of city property in Chicago which have been increasing in value at the rate of one hundred percent per day over the period of the last five years."

"Fancy that," Catherine said.

McKay put the spade back in the surrey.

"Aren't you going to fill in your hole?" she said. "Someone could walk along there on their way to the opera and break their leg."

McKay took the spade out again and filled the hole.

A mob of men armed with axes and knives had attacked the *Princess* in their absence. Axes had torn away sections of the deck railings. These now floated beside the steamboat. When McKay and his party returned to the boat, the expiring sun lit the white hull and its axe wounds, making it glow with the energy of a thunderstorm.

In the shadows, half concealed by splintered spars and debris, out of sight and hidden from attention, invisible but for its slight motion, because it was hanging, you see, hanging from a rope, Catherine was the first to see the dead lynched form, and on the sight of it she seemed to lose her mind. She wailed with a terrible resonance, and her screams came back as echoes from the surrounding warehouses.

Colin climbed on board, pushing aside splintered obstacles. "It's only the old bull," he called back. "It's only the old bull alligator."

"It's not Sewall?" McKay called.

"No."

"Where's Sewall?"

"Here," Sewall said. He was lying on the boiler deck, very badly beaten. His face was bleeding, but he rose as smartly as if he had only been down on the deck searching for a button.

Even at the sight of Sewall alive, Catherine continued weeping. "I thought you were dead," she said, sobbing. "I thought you had been hanged."

"I had a few bad moments about that myself," Sewall said. "The rope was for me, of course, but I locked myself in the

37

wheelhouse, so they strung up the 'gator instead."

The old bull turned on the end of his noose with each gentle roll of the boat. Erect, his tail trailing out on the deck, he was taller than a man. He head hung down, his mouth open. His belly glittered like ice.

"The bees saved me," Sewall told them. "I'd be as dead as the old bull is now if someone hadn't decided to interfere with the hives. I don't believe they knew what was in them. They dropped one hive, and the bees came out and stung the piss out of them. The man who dropped the hive is going to die from his stings, I know it. He must have taken a hundred stings. The bees assassinated him. We've got to put the hives right, by the way, before we do anything else."

McKay brought out the Quinby smoker, and with Colin's help he soon had it producing clouds of cool, thick smoke. they put on veils and gloves and went to work putting the hives back on their stands. The peaceful smoke made the bees forget their passion. Most of them returned to their combs. By the time the Germans arrived, the air above the steamboat's stern was a good deal less poisonous than it had been an hour before.

"Who did this?" the Germans wanted to know. People said they were a warlike race, and here they were, living up to their advertisements.

"Some good old boys from Missouri," Sewall said. "The free-soilers call them "border ruffians," but "ruffian" doesn't sound like the right word; they're naughtier than ruffians, somehow. They don't like me because I take free-soilers to Kansas, and they think Kansas ought to be a slave state, like Missouri. They think I do them a lot of damage, and that flatters me, but flattery isn't worth dying over. When I first came here, I used to enjoy riling them up, but now they're so hysterical, I'd just as soon avoid them."

"Won't they come back?"

"I'd say we were fairly safe for the time being," Sewall said. "The bees really gave them the business. And like all bullies, they can't stand pain. They'll let us leave without bothering us any more."

6

THEY STOPPED at a tree-covered island to bury the old bull.
Edward and Jiffy dug the hole, and afterward helped themselves to the raspberries growing all around. The cow alligator
sent up a dreadful alarm of shrieks and groans when she saw
her mate taken away. She could not be consoled with food,
with words, with attention. Her cries upset everyone on the
boat. At last it was decided that she should be given her freedom, since she could not be fertile without a husband. She
slipped into the water and disappeared with a powerful wiggle.

Later that day, they reached the site of Lawrence, Kansas.
Here, in the evening, McKay fell into a melancholy as black
as any he had ever experienced.

He woke Catherine in the night. They spoke together for
a while, looking at the river. The water was broad enough to

sustain waves, tiny ones, which ran into the river grass with a bright rhythm. The moon supervised all this from an improbable distance.

"I've lost my nerve," he told her. "Everything seems senseless suddenly. To be so far away from home, with you and Colin, and those bleating Germans. They're so sheeplike. They have to be provided for like farm animals."

"You drank too much whiskey."

"I didn't. I drank too little, actually. The whole population of this town went to bed without a care in the world."

"They're Sewall's friends," Catherine said. "He's Moses to them. He delivered most of them here."

"But they carried on, and on, and on. They drank and prattled. They talked too much. Did you notice how they talked and talked, and everything they said made them seem more wretched? They're all Northerners, aren't they? Northerners are supposed to be taciturn. May I put my head in your lap?"

He did this, but somehow it wasn't the comfort he imagined it would be. This comfort was beyond Catherine's flesh, beyond the graceful blemishes of light on the river, as remote and abstract as a vision of heaven, and as difficult to bring to mind.

"They're so pathetic," McKay said. "I want to weep for them and curse them in the same breath. They've been here a year, and they've accomplished nothing."

"That's not true," Catherine said. "They've built pretty little houses and started farms."

"Hovels. There isn't one building with more than a single floor. And they starved through the winter. They're all as gaunt as death."

"They seem quite cheerful."

"Oh, my," McKay said. "I don't want to be cheerful and starving a year from now. They're setting us a terrible example. Why do they want to heap themselves with trouble the way they do? They have rats, and blight, and flood, and not only

41

the border ruffians but the Missouri militia to harass them. I would find that hard to thrive on."

"The mayor wasn't pathetic at all. What was his name? It began with T. T-something. Tyler."

"No, Thayer."

"That's right, Thayer," Catherine said. "He was quite dignified."

"Sewall knew him in one of his previous lives. They were aristocrats together in Boston," McKay said. He lifted his head. He listened, but the wilderness was quiet. What did he expect to hear? Settlers tramping past in the night, racing to the new lands to establish their claims?

"You can't sit still."

"No, I can't sit still," he said, "and I can't sleep, and I can't plan, and I can't act. I feel exhausted before we've even begun, but somehow I've got to change all this. I've got to get back to the way I was. Otherwise we'll never beat the risks of this place."

Eli Thayer and his friends had incorporated themselves as the New England Emigrant Aid Company in the spring of the previous year. The articles of their incorporation permitted them to hold a capital of five million dollars, although they never at any time had a tenth of this sum. At the very moment the Nebraska Act passed Congress, they made their way to the Missouri border and walked into Kansas in the last days of July. The outrages they suffered on crossing the Missouri line, the losses of life and property, were a sorrow and a humiliation, but they were only more of the perils of travel that Thayer's grandfather and uncle, whaling captains from New Bedford, sailed in defiance of every day. Why do the fishing fleets go out every morning, regardless of the hazard? Why do they leave the coasts of Cape Cod, of Ireland, of Mull, in ice storms and fog? What is the sailor thinking as he leaves his home behind? What does he expect to find on the other side of the horizon? The perils of travel themselves must be romantic, or people would learn to live without them.

Thayer's party established itself at Lawrence, the first place they came to that was as yet free from Indian claims. Here the river was broad and shallow. The river snakes that lay in the sun on the slender grass-covered islands could be shot and eaten. The cottonwoods Thayer's company cut in clearing fields became building materials. The corn they planted grew as viciously as flowers in a rain forest. At the end of summer, they looked at the progress their town had made and were pleased. Settlers from New England and New York heard of their prosperity and came to join them.

An election was scheduled for the twenty-ninth of November to choose a delegate to Congress. This was the signal for the border counties of Missouri to prepare to send an invasion of voters. The senator from Missouri, a Mr. Atchison, encouraged these preparations in public speeches. On the day of the election, the population of the Kansas Territory doubled, and the candidate of the slaveholding interests was elected. The same outrages attended the election of the Legislature of the Territory three months later. Thayer and his friends refused even to vote in these fraudulent elections. The first act of the Legislature was to expel the only free-state candidate elected, and the second was to enact a draconian code of laws by copying over the Missouri Statute Book, changing the word "Missouri" to "Kansas" wherever it appeared. It was now an offense to be in the possession of certain Northern newspapers, or to encourage a Negro with so much as a smile.

Thayer had been a vigorous capitalist in Massachusetts, and had more than once used the power of money to bring an enemy to his knees, but he was also a man known for his charity. Charity, of course, cannot be acquired the instant one is able to afford it, but must be practiced and cultured from birth, as one would culture a musical talent. When the young Thayer brought destitute animals into his bedroom, when he collected clothes for the orphans of the Afghan war, he was preparing himself for a life in which charity would play as large a part as ambition. It was charity which brought Thayer into the early ranks of the abolitionists; charity which made him decide to emigrate to Kansas as a free-state squatter; and charity which allowed him to suppose that President Pierce was ignorant of the fraud which had overwhelmed the territorial elections. He put a pouch of tobacco and a change of underdrawers in a leather bag and set off for Washington to bring the suffering of Kansas to the attention of the federal government.

Perhaps it was romantic to make such an impulsive journey, but it was also practical to use the power and influence of his rich grandfather, and Thayer employed this persuasion skillfully to obtain an audience with the President. The chief executive was being shaved when Thayer was allowed to see him. His barber danced about, stropping razors and carrying on an intimate banter with his patron. Even in the midst of this distraction, Thayer presented his case passionately. And when he had finished describing the harassment of the mobs, the killing and the looting, and the sham of illegal voting, tears flowed from the President's eyes. The tears ran down into the shaving lather and dripped from the President's chin. They fell to the floor like drops of milk. He rose from his chair and embraced Thayer. Convulsions of sobs shook his shoulders. In a voice thick with remorse, he promised justice.

Thayer returned to his hotel a happy man. Kansas suffered under clouds of oppression, but he saw now that these clouds were only an isolated storm in an otherwise clear sky. He chided himself for ever doubting that reason and charity were more powerful than ignorance and fear. In the evening, he walked miles along the Potomac and admired the flowering trees. Only

44

the darkness and its cold brought him any memory of the hard winter past.

On the next morning, Thayer returned to the White House as he had been instructed to do. He arrived at eight, but was told by the President's appointment secretary that he rarely left his bed before ten. Toward eleven o'clock, the barber arrived with his kit of shaving supplies. Ignoring Thayer, he assaulted the appointment secretary with bullying horseplay.

"Leave me alone, Giuseppe," the appointment secretary said. He was a thin young man with a slight fuzz on his upper lip. "I'm a person, just the same as you and everyone else, and I don't have to stand for your nonsense. My brother showed me what to do the next time you started bothering me, and I swear I'll do it if I have to."

The barber disappeared through a pair of oak doors with eagles carved on them. As noon approached, Thayer wrote a note and asked to have it delivered to the President.

The secretary read the note before he rose from his chair. "What do you want to see him about?" he asked. "Are you selling something?"

"No," Thayer told him, "I am not. If you would simply deliver the message, please."

"Most of the men who come here are trying to sell him something. He buys a lot of jewelry, silk underwear, nice soaps, that sort of thing."

The note was delivered. In a short time, the barber appeared. He was no longer the exuberant character from a Rossini opera. Thayer could see that he was older than he pretended to be.

"Go away," the barber said. "The President tells you to go away and be happy he doesn't throw you in jail."

"There must be some mistake," Thayer said. "Yesterday he wept and embraced me and promised me justice."

"There's no mistake," the barber said. "Yesterday was a

45

weeping day. He wept over everything yesterday, from the affairs of the Crimea to the rip in his pajamas. Today he isn't so foolish. He considered all morning whether he should throw you in jail or whether he could risk letting you get away. His friends in the Senate have offered to pay him a bounty for every abolitionist he locks up."

The barber sat in a Chippendale chair and looked out the window. "I hate to see a man locked up for politics. In Italy, the princes locked my father up for politics, and he came back to us a white-haired crazy man. I argued for letting you go. You look harmless to me, and I told him so. I only hope to God I'm right."

7

THAYER AND MCKAY became friends quickly because they shared a glorious enthusiasm for bees. Thayer had also studied the Reverend Langstroth's book; in fact, he had twice journeyed from Boston to Colrain, Massachusetts, to visit Langstroth and question him. Thayer had a first-edition copy of *Langstroth on the Hive and the Honey-bee.* Its title page was very grandly illustrated. Below the subtitle, "A Beekeeper's Manual," was an engraved illustration of the queen on her comb. The workers surrounded her, their heads pointing toward her, so that their bodies streamed away like rays. Around the illustration, in letters which curved to touch it above and below, was printed:

EVERY GOOD MOTHER SHOULD BE THE
HONORED QUEEN OF A HAPPY FAMILY.

McKay was surprised to find himself thrilled again as he turned the pages. He opened the book to the description, which he could almost recite by heart, of the discovery of the bee-space, which Langstroth had encountered by accident. Three-eighths of an inch separated the frames from each other, from the walls of the hive body, and from the combs above and below. The bees used these spaces for passage, and left them free of combs. A smaller space they would glue shut with propolis; a larger space they would utilize for burr. It was an invention which changed everything, which made it possible now to keep bees for enormous profit.

On another page, under the heading *The honey-bee capable of being tamed or domesticated to a most surprising degree*, Langstroth described how the bees could be managed as safely and peacefully as rabbits or fowl by a beekeeper who understood how to avoid angering them. Langstroth was certain that any man who could put away his fear of stings and learn something of insect physiology could now expect to find a fortune in the culture of bees. And because he would encounter and participate in the workings of a foreign society, because he would become alert to flowers and learn their varieties, because he would learn to recognize the queen and would organize all his activities around maintaining her health, the man would find a fortune greater than the money he would earn. He would find a spiritual fortune. Langstroth said none of this explicitly, but it was there.

"He lives with his sister—a woman by the name of Margaretta Brainard," Thayer told McKay. "I didn't see him on the first visit I made to him. An illness kept him in his bed. I thought this was strange at the time, because he hadn't mentioned any illness in his letters. But he wrote and asked me to come

48

back, and so I did. I spent most of an afternoon with him last spring, just before we came here."

"How marvelous," McKay said. "It's difficult for me to visualize him as a man. I think of him as a book."

"He's very much a man," Thayer said, "although he looks like a lion. He has a great big head, and a heavy neck, and thick white hair. And he has these sort of jowls, the way lions do. He wears rimless spectacles down on the end of his nose, so that he's always looking at you over them, as if he were making a special effort to let you see his eyes. And he always wears his clerical collar and black vest, even when he's working with the bees."

"Was he pleasant to you?"

"Very pleasant indeed," Thayer said. "We sat in his sister's garden and drank tea. We began with bees, but the bees led everywhere else. He knows a great deal about classical literature, particularly Virgil. He can recite hundreds of lines of the *Aeneid*. He's also fond of mathematics, and in fact he was a tutor in mathematics at Yale before he entered the ministry. He was very interested in my reasons for emigrating to Kansas, and we talked about that. He hates slavery as much as I do."

"I would like to meet him myself," McKay said.

"I hope you do," Thayer told him. "You'll find him very sweet, as I did. He shares everything he has, which isn't much. He's quite poor, you know. This illness he has is apparently chronic, and keeps him flat on his back when it strikes him. He has twice had to resign from the ministry of a church because the illness prevented him from carrying out his duties. At the moment, he hasn't got a church. I believe he lives on the charity of his sister's husband."

"What about his book? He must be getting something from that."

"Very little, I think. He had to pay to have it published at all. He has a patent on his hive, which he took out before

49

the publication of his book, but he gave one-half the interest in all his inventions to a dentist in Greenfield in order to be able to pay for having the book printed. He sold the patent rights for the Western states and territories to a man in Wisconsin, who paid him with bad notes. And, of course, the hives are so simple to copy that it's impossible to collect royalties. I don't think he's made more than a hundred dollars from hives or bees in his whole life."

The Yankees had built Lawrence to resemble a New England village. It was a reconstruction of a whaling town, but it was in the middle of the American prairie. Where had they found the clapboards, the tall timbers for the church spires, the white paint? Perhaps they had brought all these with them from New England. The Germans admired the neat appearance of the town. "This is more like it," they said. They made an effort to be pleasant, and the people of Lawrence made an effort back, so that many friendships were begun.

Catherine was particularly welcome. She spent a great deal of time helping Thayer's wife, who was about to give birth to her first child.

"These people are extremely nice," she told her brother. "I've made up my mind to stay here until their baby is born. I've already spoken to McKay about it. Our lands are only two days further on. Someone can come back and fetch me in a fortnight or so."

"I'll do it," Colin said.

"That would suit me very well," she said.

They were speaking together in a main street. Behind them, a horse was tied to the hitching rail in front of Steiner's General Merchandise and Provisions. The horse was harnessed to a wagon containing the women and children of a silent family. None of them wore shoes. A block and tackle swung in the wind from the loft of Steiner's store.

50

"I need a short holiday from McKay," she said. "It should do us both some good."

The wind lifted Catherine's skirts, so that she had to hold them down with her hands. The rim of her bonnet fluttered. Colin and Catherine were so nearly the same height that only their clothes helped one tell them apart, and the way his shoulders came out more squarely, and the way her waist came in. Her wrists were thinner also, and her ankles.

"Aren't you going to ask me what I mean by that?"

"No," he said. "I suppose you have your reasons."

"Don't you want to know the reasons?"

"If you want to tell me."

"I don't want to tell you if you don't want to hear."

"I *do* want to hear," he said.

And so he listened as his sister explained McKay's fears of failure, his ambition, and his restlessness. McKay was extravagant with investment capital but miserly with the money he allowed for his and Catherine's maintenance. He was full of enthusiasm in public and terror in private. Everything he did was a contradiction, and he saw this himself, but did nothing to change it. Colin listened as Catherine said all this, and he never doubted the truth of it, but the knowledge seemed an imposition in the same way that lies are impositions.

In the first week of July, a message came that Catherine was ready to leave Lawrence. McKay's party had at this time been on the site of their new settlement for ten days. Colin saddled two horses and started along the track the Crow had made paralleling the Smoky Hill River down to its mouth on the Kansas.

The horses stepped in rainwater ponds warm enough to incubate eggs. There had been heavy rain the previous week, but now the sky was brilliant. The sumac were sending their flowers forward on dense panicles, often a foot long and five inches wide. Some of the tips of their branches had been killed by the heavy frosts of the winter just over. Along the banks, in the marshes, the river ash were also coming into flower. Their flowers were inconspicuous among the gray branches, four-toothed, no petals, some of them falling now under the encouragement of the wind.

The Crow had made this path, and left signs of themselves behind, mostly evidences of careless housekeeping. An antelope carcass lay alone, its white belly with its big phallus abandoned to the rodents and birds, while only the meat of the flanks and the heart had been taken. The settlers at Lawrence had met the Crow and established some rapport with them, but McKay's party had not yet seen an Indian.

Colin was pleased to be alone in this wilderness. It had somehow been his objective since coming to the West, but the opportunity to go into it had not presented itself before now. In the midst of McKay's party, he felt himself inside a container, and in fact the *Princess* had been a luxurious box with a lid, holding them together in a small space. Now he was riding into a solitude which seemed very pleasant. He saw a meadowlark alight on one of the lower branches of a seventy-foot river ash, and stopped the horses for a moment to watch it. Sweet viburnum shrubs heavy with fragrant yellowish-white flowers crowded in the thickets.

This was the wilderness, and he was having his first real meeting with it, but he did not feel frightened or peculiar in any way.

There is a common sense which can be applied to topography, and Colin had enough of this common sense to know what he would find in the land farther along. This common sense prevented him from leading the horses down blind paths that could only end in ledge outcroppings or deep pools, paths which could not possibly be the trail, although the Crow had left no overt markings to show the way. Where the river ran through marsh, the track led onto higher ground. At the margins of the marshes, abstract hedges of swamp poplar choked off the view of the water. Their branchlets were stout, roundish, varying in color, some of them rough with raised leaf scars. Their inflorescence was long past; shade cast by the green disks of their small leaves was already fusing into a general darkness within their stands.

It was in the cover of one of these poplar copses, in a place where the river flowed over ledge rock, that Colin encountered the women. These were the women of the Crow, bathing and washing their clothes. Many of them were smoking, even a young woman who waded nude in the granite shallows. She held the pipe between her teeth, but took it out of her mouth as Colin led the horses by. Her hair and her black bush were wet. The Indian women stared at him but seemed unruffled. Only their dogs took alarm and ran forward to menace the horses. Before he left their sight, as a reflex, Colin tipped his hat.

During the night, as he lay in his hammock stretched between two vertically rising black ash trees, he was disturbed by the coyotes' noise and felt the strangeness of the land for the first time in his journey.

In Lawrence, he found Catherine's mood very much improved. She was full of maternal feelings for the Thayers' baby. She brought Colin to see it in the nursery of the Thayers' house.

"I was the first one to touch him," she said. "He came out of Genevieve into my hands."

She peered into the bassinet. When her yellow hair threatened to spill forward and interfere, she tucked it into the neck of her dress. Her smile was radiant, serene.

"Everything about him is perfect," she said. "He even has little toenails and fingernails. He had them from the very first moment."

She brought the baby up and fondled it. She pressed it to

her breast. It said nothing but grasped her forefinger when she offered it.

"Do you like him?" she asked.

"Why, yes," Colin said, "although I don't suppose I'm as enthusiastic as you are."

"Men think it's undignified to love babies."

"Not at all," Colin said. "We think they're perfectly nice, and quite necessary."

"You'd love him if he was your own."

"This," he said, "is probably true."

They gathered up Catherine's belongings and accepted gifts of food from the Thayers in parting.

Outside the town, they encountered Thayer's small apiary. There were four hives arranged in a neat row in a clover field. A stand of tupelo gave shelter on the northern edge. Butterflies flew low over the field, and gave back sharp flares of light when they turned their wings in certain directions, the way individual filaments of grass flare when a pasture burns. If bees were working here, they were invisible.

"Only one of his colonies is still alive," Catherine said. "The others have died. He bought these bees from a man in Missouri who never told him they were sick."

Colin scanned the field around the entrances to the hives. The air was blue and clear above them; the bees in them were indeed dead. This study absorbed his attention for several minutes. When he looked back at Catherine, he was surprised to find her weeping.

"Don't worry," he said. "Thayer can bring them all back by raising new queens. He can divide his hives from year to year until they all have bees again. You mustn't trouble yourself about them."

"I don't care about any stupid bees," Catherine said. "I care about that baby."

Colin wanted them to ride on; he had just been through

these miles of ash and willow, and knew how far they had to travel before they would reach the place he had in mind to spend the night. But now that Catherine was weeping, a terrible turn had come to his feelings. A very old compassion for her circled him and squeezed his chest. These were feelings he hoped he had put away forever, but now they were back. They affected him profoundly, even in his sex, which threatened now to lift, even though there was no cause for it to.

They road on together for miles, but the miles only carried them deeper into a trackless emotional swamp.

Why must people's feelings always hover at poles? One is either happy or miserable, secure or threatened, in love or alone. Something had yielded in Colin to put him back in a frame of mind he thought he had escaped years ago. There was an invitation in Catherine's helplessness now, an invitation to forget their resolution to grow apart. They were only one person, after all! They had been together in the womb; perhaps they even embraced there for the first time! They were like the male and female parts of a single flower. They belonged to each other so clearly. And yet the world wanted them apart, it wanted them to separate permanently. The world wanted this for its own completely unstated reasons. It would not tolerate any less than this. There could be no thought of disobeying. It was unfair, and it was an absolute commandment.

But she was alive to him again now, in the old way. She rode ahead, so that her face was invisible, and still Colin knew she was very low. He came forward and put his coat around her shoulders. The sun was obscured behind a passing cloud. Without it, the air became cold.

Late in the afternoon, they came to a place where the steep slope down was too dangerous to ride. He helped her dismount, and led first her horse and then his own down the bank. Climbing the bank again, he saw her above him, with the sun stinging her shoulder, a dark yellow bee. It hovered around her and touched her, again and again, as he climbed. The skinny birches he used to pull himself up through the gravel were like the rungs of a ladder he was climbing into the evening clouds which framed his sister's head. Filaments of hair lifted and glowed as if an electric field acted powerfully upon them.

"I think we should stop soon, Colin," she said. "I'm afraid of the snakes. I don't want to step in places I can't see after dark."

Colin chose a sheltered cove facing to the west, where the light would be prolonged for an hour or more after the surrounding forest was dark. He brought several large stones from the river to serve as a fireplace, and began a fire before rigging the hammocks.

They warmed the stew the Thayers had given them, and ate it with buttered bread.

"I don't like the idea of sleeping in the forest," Catherine said.

"There isn't any danger. We'll be up in the trees, where nothing can reach us."

The trees he spoke of were getting their last treatment of light for the day. The hemlocks were the tallest; they were red at the top, but became abruptly dark blue at the base.

"All this is pretty enough," Catherine said, "but I'd rather be looking at it from the inside of a house. I don't really like nature."

"Of course you do," he said. "Everyone does."

They went to bed in their separate hammocks before the light was entirely gone.

It is well known that love is a disturbance of the feelings which lasts forever. Once you love someone, you always love them. This was the unhappy morass Colin and Catherine had fallen into as children.

Colin lay on his back in the hammock and looked up at the constellations. The thin silver twigs of the ash trees wiped at them, a hoary broom sweeping bright junk. Here were the stars that people wanted to see pictures in, pots and pans, the warrior, the crab, the bear who holds a snake in his mouth. Snakes. They were real enough. He knew that Catherine feared them by instinct. If you slept on the ground, they would crawl into the blankets with you, like slender, dangerous kittens.

8

McKay gave the name Equilibrium, Kansas, to his new city. Before leaving Boston, he had contracted for a hotel to be built on the new lands. It stood near completion by the time his party arrived. The river broadened into a still lake here, a quarter of a mile wide and ten miles long. From the elaborate front porch, it was possible to see several miles of the lake and its wooded islands. Low hills whose spines pointed almost due west stood on the horizon.

The hotel rose three floors above the prairie, with the lack of sense of a cactus, that plant which comes by its height merely because of an appetite for it and not because there are any neighbors to threaten it with shade. The exterior of the hotel was pale yellow, with the cornices, gutters, moldings, and other pieces of woodwork white. The slate roof had come by steamboat from quarries four hundred miles away. The carpenters who had done this work were all the male members of two generations of a large Virginia family, imported from Richmond to take the job.

Almost immediately after their arrival, McKay and Sewall went to work with the bees. They transferred the hives to a field above the lake. Here they arranged them on a gentle slope toward the south. When they opened the hives, they were dismayed to find only twelve of the original fifteen containing any living bees.

By this time, Sewall had read Langstroth's book and was familiar with Langstroth's techniques of queen management. With McKay's help, he cut out the combs until he found a living queen. He handled her as carefully as he had ever handled a life before. He put her in a queen case carved of soft pine. This queen, together with the surviving bees from the hive, he placed in a small nuclear hive which he brought into the cellar of the hotel for the night.

The next morning, he rose very early, and found that the bees had left the queen. She was chilled and stiff, and could hardly move. He took her out of the cage with fear for her life and warmed her with his breath. When she stirred and moved about in his hand, he returned her to the cage and the other bees. He watched her all day to be sure that the bees were attending her. He fed the workers honey and water on the screen of their box.

Sewall spent the night in the cellar with his queen, periodically lighting matches to ascertain her health. The following morning, when it was clear she was thriving, he came out into the sunlight.

Of the two remaining queens, one proved to be a drone layer. Sewall decided she must be replaced. He removed each frame from the hive and inspected it. When he discovered the queen, he crushed her with his finger. He replaced all of the frames containing drone eggs with empty comb, except for two. In this space he inserted two frames of fresh eggs, pollen, and honey taken from the one strong colony.

"That's all I can do for them," he said when he had finished. "They have to help themselves now."

"Are you sure you know what you're doing?" Catherine asked him.

This was after dinner, in the dining room of the hotel. The mirrors reflected candles, but they were also blue at the top because the sky still had light in it, a quarter of an hour after sunset. The Germans made conversation all but impossible with their yammering.

"I don't know quite what you mean," Sewall said to her. "I've never managed bees before, if that's your question. I've only done what Langstroth says to do in his book. It makes theoretical sense to me, what I've done, but we'll have to wait and see how it turns out in practice."

Catherine was allowing a vague and uncommitted interest in the bees to develop within her. She knew that the bees were women. They were dignified, dangerous, purposeful women. She herself had little claim to female dignity. She had no children, no family. Other women her age had these things. They knew themselves by their responsibilities. From the moment they rose in the morning, they had a purpose in all their activities, a purpose outside of themselves. But what a purpose! One would be concerned with cleaning and preparing meals perpetually! It was bondage in every way, and sealed with a ring. A ring! Symbol of pointlessness, of endless circles. And yet this was all dignified; even forest animals recognized the family as dignified.

"What have you done with them, exactly?" Catherine asked him. "You're making one hive sit on the other's eggs?"

"They don't sit on them, they feed them. They'll raise themselves a queen, by feeding some of the larvae a rich food."

Sewall's eyes reflected the candles and the silverware. The reflections disappeared as he lowered his eyes to pour tea, and returned as he looked up. "What are the bees to you?" he asked her. "How much do you want to know? I could tell you a little or keep you here all evening."

"Oh, don't do that," Catherine said. "I suppose I'm only superficially interested. McKay has got me keeping the accounts, and as the bees are in the accounts, I thought I should know something about them."

She had asked for the accounts as a distraction. She was in charge of all financial matters, and her desk held the considerable quantity of cash which McKay had brought from Boston. In keeping inventories of McKay's possessions, she would survey what the marriage had brought her. She would look into his books the way a physician looks into a patient's throat, in order to have a more intimate knowledge of him. McKay had already turned out the contents of his heart for her. Now he could show her what was in his pockets.

"My dear lady," Sewall said, "the bees are much more romantic in real life than they are in any accounts. You mustn't expect to find them as practical as they are made out to be. They have a morale which goes up and down as swiftly as yours or mine. In the late spring, when fruit flowers have just spread open, the bees are genuinely happy. They would grin, if they could. They love the world and it loves them back. But if the queen should die or fall ill, they trouble themselves about it so much that they can't work."

Sewall spread a piece of bread with butter and put it in his mouth. The lines around his mouth became folds and then lines again as he chewed. An old man in a young country. And yet there was nothing compromised about his strength. He was taller and more powerful than either Colin or McKay.

"The bees are every bit as emotional as people, and it does them quite as much harm. In that respect, they're not like wild creatures at all. They're like us, and that makes me sorry for them, I suppose," he said.

Catherine looked into her cup without answering.

The hotel was within a romantic landscape, and this pleased the Germans very much. They put on their wandering boots and explored the surrounding countryside thoroughly. They walked through the fields recently cleared for agriculture. They discovered a waterfall above the north end of the lake, and climbed the hills which were visible from the front porch of the hotel.

"This is such a luxurious country," Mrs. Finger told McKay. "Everywhere you walk, you must watch your feet to make sure you don't fall over a berry bush. You can shoot a deer or a fat pigeon by accident, simply by firing your gun in any direction. The little waterfall is more beautiful than any I have seen in the Alps. This place would be a vision of heaven if it weren't for the dirty Indians."

The Germans thought the Indians were dirty because they had come upon a party of young people copulating in the woods. They had not recognized what was going on until they had come quite close. The Indians were in positions the Germans had never imagined would be practical for the purpose, and they were having their intercourse with their clothes on. The men had simply drawn their loincloths aside like curtains, and the women had lifted their skirts. None of the Indians paid the Germans the slightest attention, or even acknowledged their presence. The women returned the males' thrusts blow for blow, slowly and mechanically, as if they were taking part in a ritual work operation, perhaps the shucking of corn. The Germans ran away, shrieking with righteous rage.

Catherine could see that McKay was at last at ease. He was in the carpenter shop and the fields all morning, supervising the construction and management of the growing apiary. At noon he would stride boisterously into the dining room, bragging about the success the bees were having with the sweet clover which was now coming into bloom everywhere, and would drink too much wine with his lunch. The wine bottles would be sticky afterward, because he and Sewall were now harvesting their first honey. The white clover nectar was so abundant that the bees in the strong hives could fill a super with thirty pounds of capped honey in four days.

McKay would often sleep through the afternoon, spread on the velvet coverlets wearing all his clothes, even his shoes, under the white glare of the windows.

Edward and Jiffy had undertaken an extensive vegetable garden behind the hotel. The space had been plowed for them, but they were still obliged to break up the sod and remove the stones which littered the ground. The boys had done this work for their mother at home, and were proficient at it. When the seed bed was prepared, they planted carrots, onions, potatoes, turnips, spinach, tomatoes, lettuce and kale. Each day they carried water from the river in buckets to irrigate their garden. When the shoots began to show through the ground, they built a solid fence five feet high to keep the rabbits out. They controlled the weeds with patience and devotion.

In the midst of all this progress, Catherine was unhappy. Everyone else was involved in hand-to-hand combat with the land. McKay and Sewall were fully occupied with the bees. The Germans were building hives and making patterns for their music boxes. Colin had begun his surveying. She was keeping the accounts, but this was only a spectator's job, watching what other people did and writing it down. It wasn't enough.

When she was younger, on a holiday trip to the south of France, she had learned to make earthen pots. The clay was marvelously fine and smooth, as if it had been enriched with animal cells. It was cold and stiff before it was worked, but became plastic and lifelike the more it was beaten. After you had formed it just the way you wanted, you put it in an oven and baked it, like food. But whereas food becomes soft with cooking, clay becomes hard. It turns to stone.

Catherine had been told her pots were good. She knew this herself. Now she had a strong wish to take up pottery again.

When she told Colin her feelings, he put away his surveying tools and set about building her a kiln. He went into the carpenter's shop and made brick molds. He experimented with drying his bricks in the sun, but finally decided to fire them in the blacksmith's forge. He worked for more than a week making bricks, and when he judged that he had a sufficient number, he began construction of the kiln. He made its oven large enough to accommodate pots four feet high. The firebox would take logs as long as a man's leg. He built a tall chimney to insure a good draft, and borrowed an iron firebox door from the *Princess*.

The finished kiln was plain, but it worked well. Colin baked it out with a fire he kept white hot for days. Catherine's expectations for herself and the things she could do rose like the superheated air in the chimney. She stood by the furnace and felt its invisible heat. The sound was reminiscent of a waterfall, but here was a waterfall which flowed up instead of down. The sound vibrated her chest. It was a feeling like singing. Colin had made it for her, this bright furnace which shook the ground. It was her tool, and it was very dignified. She was filled with love for Colin.

"Come look at this," Sewall said to her. He led her to a corner of Edward and Jiffy's garden. With his hands on his hips, he searched the ground, apparently judging the pea shoots. He reached down and picked up a dead bee.

"Here he is," he said. "I saw him falling out of the sky a

moment ago, coming straight down like a stone, and I knew what had happened."

"What's the matter with it?" Catherine asked.

"This is a drone," Sewall told her. "It's an eviscerated drone, actually. He has just had sex with one of my young queens. They go up together in a wedding flight, and he takes her in the air. His penis is torn away in the process. His bowels and most of the contents of his abdomen are lost as they separate. The brother mates with his sister, and dies afterward."

9

GENEVIEVE THAYER was a Missouri girl. She had married Eli Thayer in order to spite her parents and get away from Lock Springs, Missouri, where she felt her heart being eaten from below the way a tomato is eaten when it brushes the ground. She was a pretty girl, popular with her peers, but at the age of eighteen she knew she must do something outrageous enough to bring her reputation past a certain threshold. If she failed to do this, she could expect to sink into paralyzing obscurity, and live on a social plane lower than the worms. But if she succeeded, she would be entitled to lasting respect. "That's Linda Sue Turney," Lock Springs people still said of a woman with no teeth. "She's the one who got drunk with a soldier at her sister's wedding and afterward lived with him in his tent."

Between her sixteenth and eighteenth years, the traditional age for hardening off one's reputation, Genevieve considered and rejected smoking in church, stealing from the mercantile store, and burning her father's house down, but when at last a Massachusetts man came through leading a party of abolitionists, she threw herself at him.

The spleen of the town came forward in a gush less than a day after she had said her first word to him. Her parents were so angry and frightened that they shut her in her room at the top of the house. When an opportunity came for her to steal away to him in the darkness, she crept from the town with mixed feelings, knowing on the one hand that the achievement would drive a knife through the heart of every competitor she had ever had, and on the other that, now she was leaving Lock Springs, she might never know the full extent of her notoriety.

At first, marriage with Eli Thayer seemed curiously placid to her. People said such terrible things about Yankees, she expected that life with a devil would be full of nettles and thunderclaps. She had heard that Yankee men were selfish and dishonest, but Thayer was none of these things. If he said he was going out in the evening for a certain purpose, and she asked casual questions the next day to check his story, it was always possible to verify that he had been telling the truth. He shared his money with her and never complained when she bought herself clothes. He even read the Bible, although she suspected that he didn't really feel his religion. She felt herself changing to become like him in ways she never dreamed of.

He built a pretty house for them in Lawrence, and got himself elected mayor. Things seemed very satisfactory indeed, and she never thought of Lock Springs or any of the people there for months at a time.

Most of this changed when the baby was born. It seemed

67

to need all her tenderness. When she was finished feeding it, and bathing it, and washing its clothes, she only wanted to be alone. She unbuttoned herself to the baby now, and to no one else. She gave it her warmth, more warmth than she knew she had. It needed every bit. This was as natural as could be, and why should she be made to feel guilty about it? But she did feel guilty from time to time, because her husband had almost disappeared for her. He just wasn't there.

"Are you coming to dinner at the table, or do you want to be spoon fed?" she called to him one time.

He had been reclining in a large chair in the parlor. "I want to be spoon fed," he said. "No, breast fed."

She had moved about silently in the kitchen without speaking, deeply offended. Tears had welled in her eyes. Leaving his beans to incinerate in the oven, she had gone up the back stairs to the bedroom, closing the door behind her.

Thayer had followed her. He sat down gently on the edge of the bed. "I was only joking," he said. He stroked her hair, but she pulled away. "I was only joking, Genevieve."

"You were not. It's what you really want. You're jealous of the baby."

"That's not true," Thayer said. "It really isn't true."

"Yes it is. You see me taking care of the baby and you want the same thing. You can't bear to see the baby getting something you're not. You're just a big baby yourself."

"For Christ's sake," Thayer said. "I was just making a joke."

"It wasn't any joke," she said. "None of this is any joke. I hate Lawrence. I hate you. I hate baked beans. Nobody ever said anything about baked beans before we were married."

"I didn't know you hated baked beans," Thayer said. "If you don't like them, we won't have them any more."

"Oh, it isn't only that," Genevieve said, sobbing. "It's everything, it's everything."

She made up her mind to leave him. She packed a trunk

for the baby and herself and got on a steamboat.

In Kansas City, she hired a man with a wagon to drive her to her mother's house in Lock Springs. On the way, she asked him many questions about Lock Springs people he didn't know. As they approached the town, she clutched her baby close and pointed out familiar sights. There was the schoolhouse and there was the peach tree she had fallen out of and broken her arm. Children were playing bull-and-pony on the courthouse lawn, and as she drove by, she saw a girl among them as much like herself as an old portrait. Seeing this girl was like recognizing herself in the middle of a summer day in her youth, and her feelings leapt the whole distance into that simple happiness.

"They all have babies now," her mother said when they were alone. Genevieve's father had paid the man with the wagon and was supervising the Negroes moving her trunk up the stairs to the top of the house. "All the girls you went to school with have babies, even the plainest ones. Do you remember May Ellen Farley, the heavy girl with all the freckles? We thought she'd never get a man, but her father took a simple fellow from South Lock Springs into his lumber business and he gave her a baby. At night, when she thought no one could see her, she'd hang by her knees from the swings in the schoolyard and shake all over, trying to get rid of it. I watched her from this porch, night after night, wriggling like a snake, but it didn't work and she had to marry the idiot."

The house where Genevieve had been born and raised was almost as vast as the mercantile store where her father sold the iron goods, timber, hay, and other provisions which made him one of the town's wealthiest merchants. A wide porch ran around three sides of the house, so that entering by any door meant crossing the porch. Tupelos climbed by the south side of the house for its full three floors. When the Negroes painted the house every third year, they could stand in the

69

boughs of the tupelo trees and reach the clapboards with long-handled brushes.

Genevieve sat with her mother on the porch and listened to her account of the fortunes of the people of Lock Springs. A cyclone had come to the edge of the town during the previous summer, but had been turned away by crazy old Mr. Billings, who had chased it with a scythe. His wife had seen blood falling out of the cyclone as he chased it away. A child had been born in the town with short arms and tiny little hands no bigger than violets, and people said that this meant there was incest nearby. Bucky Dragon's father had died, leaving him the whole plantation, and the old man hadn't been cold a day before his son had taken most of his father's savings to buy polo ponies.

Her mother's mention of Bucky Dragon brought Genevieve a deep stir in her feelings. They had been lovers once, and had sat together on this porch and fanned each other with green tobacco leaves. They were the same age. Bucky Dragon had been on intimate terms with every young woman in the county, married or not, but somehow it was widely assumed that he and Genevieve would eventually marry. This was assumed because only he was handsome enough for her, and only she was fair enough for him. They matched each other in every important way—each had a well-developed sense of mischief, a short temper, an appreciation of pedigree. Lock Springs people recognized that it was natural for Bucky Dragon to want to stick his thumb into every pie in the county before he made up his mind to take a wife, but they were certain that when the time came, he would choose Genevieve.

This widespread assumption, that Bucky and Genevieve were destined for each other, had been a comfortable knowledge for Genevieve's mother. It was a certain knowledge of the future—like the certain knowledge of the coming positions of the stars that makes long sea voyages possible. Is the State Legislature planning to tax and regulate the sale of whiskey?

70

When Genevieve and Bucky are married, Bucky's uncle will see that it is possible for Genevieve's father to get a liquor license. Has old Mrs. Graves blocked the nomination of Genevieve's mother to the governing board of the Historical Society? When Genevieve and Bucky are living in the Big House on the Dragon plantation, she will arrange a meeting of the Society in the West Library, the oldest structure in central Missouri, built by Josiah Dragon with his own hands in 1751, and old Mrs. Graves will be turned away from the door.

This vision of the future still seemed real to Genevieve's mother. The business about Genevieve running away to Kansas with a pack of abolitionists was so improbable, so unnatural, so unfair, that she could only treat it as a bad dream.

"Your Italian velvet finally came," she told her daughter. "I put it up in your room for you. Daddy said I was being foolish, but I knew you were coming back. I put it with your sewing things. You can finish the pillows for your hope chest now. Perhaps I'll help you do it, later, if I'm not feeling too tired."

In the evening Genevieve escorted her sister to the Masons' dance. A full year had passed since she had set foot in the town. A young child of her own lay asleep at her mother's house in the very cradle she had used as a baby, but somehow all this recent past was forgotten, mown down, and carried off the way hay is taken out of a field in June, making it ready for a whole new growth.

As they passed the schoolyard, Genevieve's sister suggested they go in for a smoke. They sat under the heavy red oaks, keeping the trunks between them and the street. The canopy above was so thick that it let not a single star shine down.

Genevieve's sister brought a cigar out of her lace purse and lit it. "Homer gets these for me," she said. "He takes them from his daddy's desk. I didn't like to smoke when I first tried, but Homer made me do it again and again, and finally I liked it. I remember when you first started smoking. Mama found that cigar butt in your purse, and she made you eat that teaspoon of Daddy's pipe tobacco. I was so frightened. I thought with the way you were throwing up and all that maybe you were going to die, but I believed Mama was right for making you do it. I believed smoking was a terrible sin, and she had to cure you. Isn't that ridiculous? I was so stupid then, and little. I didn't even have my breasts."

The dance was held in the Masonic Temple, a brick building whose second-story windows were always dark, even in the daytime, so that the spaces behind the glass seemed perpetually in winter. Now the first floor was lit by purple lamps, but even their light was cold, like the light one expects of electric creatures who live in the sea. Genevieve and her sister paid their admission to Mr. Thompson, who owned the grocery across from their father's hardware.

"Now you bring that youngster into the store tomorrow," he said to Genevieve. "You bring him in, and we'll see if there isn't something he likes in one of my candy jars. I'm your father's friend, and you broke his heart, but Jesus teaches us to forgive. The Chink put up a sign in front of his laundry—really, you wouldn't believe it, gaudy colors and the poorest taste imaginable, just like he owns the street—but I forgive him. Old man Willis hasn't paid his bill in two years, and last week he comes in and orders up this, that, and the other sent to his house, and talks about what a good customer he is. If I can forgive him, I guess I can forgive you. My wife told me to make a special point of inviting you into the store. She thinks that if we're real nice to you, maybe you'll learn to love your own Christian white folks as much as you love the niggers."

Inside, Genevieve scanned the faces of the dancers to find people she knew. Most were years younger than herself, and therefore unknown to her. This was the same hall in which,

72

a year ago, she would have known the name of every person present, and would have met opportunities for gossip and flirtation as various as the town allowed by taking a few steps in any direction. But a circle of acquaintances is the most miniature of all climates, smaller than the most isolated summer shower, and when one leaves a social climate, the fragments disperse and never come together in the same way again. Genevieve among the younger brothers and sisters of her friends was among strangers.

When the dancing resumed, her sister was led away by Homer, a slight fellow with poor skin who did not seem to recognize Genevieve at all. As the evening went on, Genevieve was asked to dance by callow youths whose voices were still changing. She joined the squares, and expected on each grand right and left to meet someone she knew, to startle him with her handshake, to frighten him with her hair flying and her mouth open and her teeth flashing, to strike him with her hoofs like a wild horse and then run on, but it never happened. She moved through the circles clasping hands with strangers. Only the rough-hewn beams in the ceiling and the purple lights in the windows were her friends. They had seen her here before, at a time in her life when she had been magnificent.

Once, standing beside the punch bowl waiting to be served, she wondered how many people in the town believed she had run away to Kansas because she loved niggers.

She walked her sister home in the dark. Homer insisted on accompanying them. He showed them some interesting mumbletypeg tricks with his pocketknife. He could balance the knife in the palm of his hand, and he could make it hop from one finger to another. He could balance it on the end of his nose. Genevieve's sister had seen all this before and was tired of it. She sent him off.

"I hate him when he starts fooling with his knife," she said. "Sometimes I think he'll never grow up. I wouldn't keep him

73

five minutes if there was anyone better, but there isn't. When I think of what you and Bucky were doing at our age, riding around the county on stolen horses, drinking corn liquor until you fell asleep in haystacks and silos, it makes me wish I'd never been born."

Genevieve was amused to hear this. Who was doing her the favor of constructing stories about her past? Which old women labored behind drawn shades to defame her character, and only added to her legend? When offered alternatives, what do people choose to believe and what makes them believe it?

After midnight, Genevieve heard horses on the lawn and knew that he had finally come. She lay awake in bed listening to the animals snorting and shifting their weight. She went to the window. Three men on horseback stood on the lawn. Bucky Dragon dismounted. The bottle in his hand flashed. He set it down carefully on the lawn and opened his trousers. He took his silvery penis in his hand and watered the honeysuckle beside the house. The honeysuckle leaves rattled under the heavy jet.

"You stop that," Genevieve called down to him. "You stop that and go away."

He staggered back, still unbuttoned. He looked up at the side of the house, but didn't see her.

"There she is," one of the men said.

10

WILLIAM SEWALL was particularly crazy about beetles. He knocked apart rotten logs for them, he looked under rocks, he thrust his collecting trowel deep into their tunnels, looking for the grubs. The detail and complexity of beetles was more strange and wonderful to him than the detail and complexity of music, or of clouds. In ponds and streams, he collected the aquatic haliplids and the predaceous diving beetles, the Dytiscidae. In pools, he found whirligigs rushing around and around each other, tracing neat circles with their speed and sending surface tension waves to each other. But his favorites were the graceful and beautiful tiger beetles, the most agile of all the families. He collected them on hot days along the stream banks and on the dirt paths the Indians made. They would remain perfectly still and allow him to come very close, and then, just before he came within reach, fly up abruptly and land ten yards farther on.

He made a game of elaborating the species of beetles to be found in a limited space. In Edward and Jiffy's garden alone, he found thirty-seven species. Within the range of a hundred feet of the hotel in any direction, he found more than fifty. If he extended his circle to a half-mile radius, his number of beetle species exceeded two hundred. In this larger circle, he found more than eighty species of tiger beetle alone. The rapaciousness of the larvae of these tiger beetles astounded him. They lived in vertical burrows in sandy places or on beaten paths. The larva assumed a position of watchfulness at the mouth of its burrow, its jaws wide open, and when an insect walked by, it struck. On the fifth segment of the abdomen, two hooks curved forward, and these hooks dug into the earth and kept the little rascal from being pulled out of its burrow when it got some large insect by the leg.

Sewall gave Catherine a demonstration of how the little fellows caught their food. He put a straw down into one of their burrows, then dug it out with his trowel. At the end was a grub about as long as a fingernail, showing the straw no mercy.

"What a nasty worm," Catherine said. "If I was that ugly, I don't think I'd dare to be that nasty."

"It's all a part of growing up," Sewall told her.

If fifty species could be found in an acre, and two hundred could be found in a square mile, Sewall estimated that half a million different species of beetle were lurking in the bushes within a day's ride of the hotel. The thought thrilled him, but also intimidated him, since the capture and identification of half a million species of beetle was a good deal more than a life's work for one man. The more he thought about the unknown beetles, and the larger he drew the perimeters of his projected beetle exploration, the more uncomfortable he became. The cold fact, which he knew he must confront, was that the structure and complexity of beetles in Kansas was too vast, too rich, too detailed, too marvelous, for any one person, even a team of a hundred people, to discover in a lifetime.

As a young man, I would have tried, he thought. But I'm not young now. The blood used to pump in my ears and I used to wear my shirt open to the navel, but not any more. He put the thought of millions of unknown beetles out of his mind.

He did, however, lead an expedition of several days to explore the geography to the west of the hotel. McKay, Colin, Edward, and Jiffy went with him. They loaded six packhorses with provisions and set off. Their route followed the bed of the Smoky Hill River, with short excursions north and south into the prairie. Except for isolated stands of trees in the bottomland of the river, they had left the great eastern hardwood forest behind. Ash, scrub oak, and cottonwood now gave way to sagebrush. The ground was covered with dry range grass. In some places, the buffalo dung was so thick that one was obliged either to step in it or shovel it to one side.

"The Crow kill those things with arrows and clubs," McKay said. They had stopped to wait for a herd of buffalo to wade out of the river and run away. "I think I'd want a howitzer to do the job, myself."

"The Crow have a lot of balls," Sewall agreed.

Whenever they left the river, they followed a precise compass course in order to avoid becoming lost. There were no mountains, no distinctive natural formations, virtually no landmarks. This was late summer, and the ground was dry, but the range grass appeared to be healthy in spite of the heat. Some afternoons, the sky would suddenly darken and a violent thunderstorm would break the morning's drought.

"Well, you couldn't grow bananas here," McKay said. "Perhaps wheat."

"Or beef," Sewall said.

The thunderstorms were absolutely brilliant with lightning. When they came in the evening, as they often did, the distant electrical displays would look like dawn on the horizon. The coyotes were invariably frightened and would set up a terrible howling, as if this were the first natural electricity they had ever seen. A big wind would come first, blowing the weeds over the ground, and then the flashes. The cowls of the tents would heave as if a tide had come in upon them. The embers of the campfire would glow white hot, and burning bits of wood would be blown into the grass, sending Edward and Jiffy after them in alarm, but the rain would always follow quickly. Once in a while, hailstones came mixed with the rain.

Sewall filled his collecting boxes with flowering grasses and butterflies, but the beetles still distracted him powerfully. He had never before captured or even seen any of the genus Brachinus, the bombardier beetles, but now he encountered a community of them. These beetles, like many others, carry at the hind end of their body little sacs in which a bad-smelling fluid is secreted. The fluid may be released for defense against other insects, but in the case of the bombardier beetles the fluid changes to a gas within the sac, and escapes with the sound of a gun. The vapor which issues out after the explosion even looks like smoke. After the beetle has created an explosion in the face of his attacker and blinded him with smoke, he runs away. Sewall captured six specimens of Brachinus one fortunate afternoon, and was shot at thousands of times for his trouble.

He saw beetles everywhere without looking for them. If he was examining some plant specimen, if he was pitching his tent, if he was cleaning the buffalo dung from his boots with a stick, he would be sure to notice some rare and strange beetle darting out of sight into the grass. At last he admitted to himself that his earlier estimate of five hundred thousand beetle species in Kansas was probably gravely in error: there could be many millions.

During the summer, the Crow came boldly forward to accept the gifts which were offered to them. Since they had been acquainted for nearly two years with the settlers at Lawrence, they knew what they wanted in the way of manufactured goods. They were particularly pleased with saucepans, and wanted as many of these as could be supplied. They used the saucepans as giant spoons, and drank their gravies and blood porridges from them.

The Crow were fascinated with the hives, and with the honey which was now being harvested from them. They had apparently never made the discovery of a bee tree, and therefore had never tasted honey. They deluded themselves into believing it was an intoxicating liquor, and acted happily drunk after eating so much as a thimbleful. When any operations were being done with the bees, they stood around and watched solemnly. They knew the bees were capable of stinging, and therefore gave the hives wide berth, but nevertheless developed an appetite for the sight of the bees at work, which brought them back as surely as their appetite for honey. They delegated one of their young men to learn to become a beekeeper, and he made excellent progress.

When the nectar flow from white clover was at an end, Sewall and McKay determined to increase their number of hives by Langstroth's method of nucleus swarming. Until this time, they had been fortunate enough to have no swarms issue from any hive. This pleased them, because in the process of swarming, the new queen takes with her a portion of the strength of the hive in the bees which follow her. Sewall had very cautiously managed the hives to prevent swarming and thus keep every bee at work until the major summer honey flow was over, but now he set about producing an artificial swarming which would multiply the number of colonies.

Twelve days before he estimated the white clover harvest would end, he set two hives to rearing queens. He looked over the frames of what seemed to be the two strongest, most prosperous hives, found the queens, and beheaded them. With a sharp knife, he cut off a portion of the lower and side margins of the combs, and then cut deep notches. These cuts insured that empty spaces were brought right among the eggs and larvae, thus giving the bees excellent conditions for the construction of queen cells. Four of these frames were put back into the hives, along with three frames of empty comb. Since all the bees were crowded on these seven frames, the hive now felt smaller to them, and they put their minds to raising queens. Six days after he put the combs in, he found twenty-seven queen cells in one hive and thirty-five in the other.

As soon as the clover harvest was finished, he divided the twelve hives which had survived the journey from New Orleans into forty-eight three-frame nuclei. Twelve of these were left with their original queens and given empty frames to replace the frames of hatching brood taken from them. The empty frames were alternated with full frames to encourage the bees to draw out the comb as soon as possible. Each of the new colonies was given one queen cell grafted into a patch of hatching brood. He now fed the hives abundantly with honey. As the combs were nearly filled with brood, the bees had no room to store this food, and were therefore encouraged to build comb in the empty frames. The weather was warm, which encouraged them further in their comb building. At the end of twenty days, still several weeks safely ahead of the fall-flower honey flow, Sewall had multiplied the original number of hives by four, and each one was swelling its strength of bees daily.

McKay was extremely proud of this success. He wrote a letter to Langstroth congratulating him on his book and giving details on the honey-farming conditions he had encountered in Kansas. Langstroth sent a reply, and this began a correspondence which was to keep McKay happily occupied throughout the fall.

In late September, Edward and Jiffy took a luxurious harvest of vegetables from their garden. Mrs. Finger and several of her cronies began a program of preserving tomatoes, beans, peas, carrots, squash, turnips, corn, and berries in glass jars.

The summer's harvest of honey was also prepared for shipment now. This was a time in our history when food was routinely adulterated. Sausages were extended with cereals, and cereals were extended with sawdust. Honey was so easily adulterated with water and corn syrup that no market existed for it except in the comb, where the purchaser could see that it had been packaged and sealed by the bees. For this reason, after the fall-flower nectar flow had ended, Sewall and McKay fed the entire one thousand pounds of honey they had extracted during the summer back to the bees, who immediately stored it away in splendid white combs. The Germans had produced their own harvest of hardwood boxes in the woodworking shop, and these now received the comb honey, three pounds at a time.

The original plan had been to take the honey to market aboard the *Princess,* but now as the crop was ready the steamboat was not. The level of the river had begun falling in July, leaving the *Princess* sitting on dry land since the middle of August. Her paddle wheels hung in the air and turned like windmills when the breezes blew through them. Everyone waited for the fall rains to come and fill the river, but somehow the sky remained cloudless. Finally, McKay hired wagons in Kansas City to come and take the crop away.

By the time the last of the honey was packaged and taken to market, the Germans were producing their first music boxes. Without asking for any opinions, they had developed a model which played "Old Dog Tray" slowly and solemnly, as a carved darkie pirouetted on top. Sewall was offended by it, but the Germans pointed out that it could be produced inexpensively and was guaranteed a large sale in Missouri, so McKay told them to go ahead.

Everyone thought that there ought to be some sort of celebration to mark the end of the gloriously productive summer. Enthusiasm for this idea spread like a disease bacillus in a kissing game. Mrs. Finger supervised the preparations for a feast. Catherine manufactured several ornamental crocks, which were filled with fruit, flowers, and honey. The Crow were invited, and brought buffalo meat. Colin constructed a large hot-air balloon.

It was sewn together from the silk panels of formal dresses Catherine said she no longer had any occasion to wear. Colin carefully fitted the panels together, day after day. He did most of this work on the front porch of the hotel, where a breeze from the river came up the slope to provide refreshment. The German ladies took turns helping him make the thousands of stitches which went into the finished product. The silk was first cut, according to a wooden pattern, into triangles, and the triangles assembled into pentagons, and the pentagons finally sewn into a sphere. A birchwood ring with ornate carvings formed the mouth. As the bag neared completion, the wind investigated its purpose from time to time by inflating it in the hands of the sewers.

The German ladies insisted that the balloon should have some sort of decoration, and sent Colin off in the company of Edward and Jiffy to buy colorful silks and braids. Edward and Jiffy knew where these might be available in Missouri. In Higginsville, they stopped for a luncheon of country sausage and corn bread at a small general store. They took their meal outdoors under a tree. A slave auction was in progress nearby. The Negroes were kept naked in a pen, where prospective purchasers were admitted to examine them. While they ate, a young woman was being sold from the tailgate of a wagon. She offered no resistance to having her mouth forced open or her bare breasts manipulated for the convenience of the purchasers, but when the bidding began, she recognized someone in the crowd and spoke to him in a loud voice.

"Don't you bid on me, Randy Billings," she said. "If you buy me, I'll stick a knife in my own heart. I knew you since we were little together. You can't buy me. That's too terrible."

On the day of the feast, the balloon was positioned on a stage above the chimney of Catherine's kiln. Toward evening, when the Germans were partly drunk and the Indians entirely so, Colin lit a fire in the firebox. The balloon inflated wearily, stretching out to its full shape like an animal which sleeps in the day but flies at night. In the last evening light, as the air within it grew hot enough almost to set it on fire, it strained against its anchor. As well as the embroidery, the German ladies had stitched a motto to the side in gold letters five feet high: PAX.

Colin climbed the ladder to the stage and set it free. From a distance, he looked like a small boy beginning some mischief. The guests roared. As it ascended, the balloon was illuminated from below by the light of flames escaping from the chimney.

11

IN LATE OCTOBER, Sewall discovered a disease of the bee brood in several of the hives. He had been suspicious when, toward the end of the summer, these colonies had suddenly lost their strength. Now he had clear evidence that they were sick. Patches of the brood were a foul brown color, sticky to the touch, and productive of an unpleasant odor. The larvae in these cells were all dead.

"Do you suppose they caught it from Thayer's bees?" Catherine asked. "How could they? Thayer's hives are fifty miles away."

"I don't know," Sewall said. "It beats me."

McKay wrote a letter to Langstroth in which he described the symptoms and asked for advice. The letter remained unanswered for over a month. Meanwhile, the disease ravaged the colonies where it had been discovered, and started in one additional hive.

"We'd better quarantine the bastards," Sewall said. "It may not help, but I feel like trying almost anything."

They decided to take the hives which were not yet infected across the river to the narrow islands where the snakes lived. These islands were close to the opposite shore, where the bees could find plentiful pasturage among the trees and flowers of the riverbank when spring came. The air was now so cold that the bees had formed their winter clusters within the hives.

There were forty-eight hives to be moved. If the river had been high enough, the bees might have traveled by boat, but in fact it was so low that the snake islands were ringed by mud flats. Black ash and river maple along the banks were now dropping their leaves into the water. The leaves floated in idle rafts, or fell in muddy places and made the bog look like hard ground. Winter was coming. The sky was transparent. A cold, extreme blue stood overhead day after day.

Sewall loaded a number of hives on a buckboard wagon and drove it into the river. The horses strained against the mud. He let them pick their way among the rocks and weeds. They waded past the steamboat. He was wearing his black and red wool jacket, and the colors reflected with perfect fidelity from the surface of the water. Although he was some distance out, it was possible to hear the water splashing as the wheels turned. Every word of encouragement he gave the horses was clear also.

He wandered up and down for the best part of an hour looking for a way through the swift channel. Once he stopped to rest the horses on a dry bar covered with range grass. For several minutes, the plume from his pipe rose straight up. Then he was off again, and the water came up over his hubs.

Finally the wagon stopped for good. "Piss on it," he said, and called for help. On the riverbank, the Crow laughed. It was a strange sight to see a wagon and team where a boat should have been. The hives were removed from the buckboard and carried to shore. Only with a great deal of effort from men and animals was the wagon freed and driven out.

The Crow watched as Colin waded in the river and surveyed the problem of moving the bees across it. The water in the main channel was moving with the speed of a fast horse. It would be possible to use a boat for this segment, but the hives would have to be carried through the mud for some distance on either side. He arranged a rope handrail suspended on poles across the full breadth of the river. The flat-bottomed boat which was to be the ferry across the deep segment was attached to the handrail through a ring at its bow.

"Haven't they got anything better to do?" Catherine asked.

"Haven't who got anything better do do?"

"The Crow," she said. "They just sit there picking insects out of their hair, watching you."

"I'm an interesting person to look at," Colin said.

He tried his handrail bridge with an empty hive strapped to his back. He found the footing awkward in some places, and the transfer of the hives into the boat was difficult, but he judged that the operation would be more manageable with several people. His legs were numbed by exposure to the cold water, and his genitals made an effort to disappear into his abdomen.

"I don't much like this arrangement," he said. "We should really take the time to build a proper bridge downstream somewhere in a narrow place."

"The weather is getting colder all the time," McKay told him. "How would you like to be wading in the water, building your bridge a month from now when the snow is coming down?"

Colin prepared a sling with shoulder straps for everyone who was to take part in the project. Each person would carry the two brood chambers of one complete hive, a weight of nearly a hundred pounds. Colin was the first across with his load, followed by Edward. Jiffy came next, but he was less successful. Before he even reached the pole where the boat was tied, he stepped in a deep place and lost his balance. With the bees tied to his back, he sat down in the river. The brood chambers came apart and the bees escaped like flames from an explosion.

The fear on Jiffy's face would not admit of description. He pulled the straps from his shoulders and ran toward the shore. The bees stung him very badly. Sewall hastened into the water with the smoker and enveloped him in a cloud of smoke. From within his smoky shroud, Jiffy wept. He seemed hysterical. Sewall led him onto the bank and removed his shirt. Working quickly, he extracted most of the stingers before they had finished injecting their venom. Jiffy lay on the bank and sobbed. His brother, on the opposite shore, was very distressed. Some of the bees still hovered around Jiffy's back, and when they came too close, Sewall let loose great white puffs of smoke. Jiffy coughed like a fire victim. The Crow snickered, perhaps from embarrassment. Most of the bees flew around the half-sunken ruins of their home.

"I'd like to crack a few of those feathered heads together," Sewall said.

"Don't," McKay told him. "It's not worth starting a war over."

Jiffy was taken into the hotel, where mud plasters were made for his stings. An overcast had moved across the sky, filling it with a cold glare. The white oak trees along the banks had refused to drop their leaves, even though every leaf had turned brown and dry. The rattling of these leaves sounded like the warnings of snakes. The Crow hung around and threw stones in the water. They were trying to hit the wreckage of the hive, but it was too far away.

"They certainly make the noble savage idea look like a lot of rubbish," McKay said. "Other people get noble savages, and we get the silly ones."

The Crow disappeared for a few hours, but returned later in the afternoon carrying the mirror which had been a gift from McKay's party earlier in the year. They carried this mirror into the river and pretended to float it on the surface. With their fingers, they showed how anyone at all might walk over the water in the coming months when it froze to ice.

12

McKay's party knew about ice, of course, and felt quite foolish at having to be told of its existence by savages. Only five weeks after Jiffy dropped the hive, a spell of cold weather froze the river solidly enough that all the disease-free hives could be moved to the snake islands aboard wagons. A clearing was made on the longest island, and a new apiary was set up, facing south.

McKay wrote more letters to Langstroth and received more silence in reply. He maintained a postal box in Kansas City and sent a regular messenger to check its contents, but it was always empty. He was certain that the border ruffians were intercepting his letters and putting the match to them. What had he done to offend these brutes? Why had they marked him as an enemy? Nothing he received in the mail seemed at all identified with abolitionist sentiment, but the Southerners were changing their definition of offensive literature every day. As a precaution, McKay canceled Catherine's subscription to the *Saturday Evening Post.*

In his alarm over the bee disease, he rode to Lawrence and brought Eli Thayer back to advise him. Thayer was now enjoying a bit of domestic tranquillity. Genevieve had returned, and no longer mentioned Lock Springs or any of its people.

Colin and Catherine went with them as they inspected the hives. They visited the diseased hives first, and found no sign of life. Thayer flattened his ear against the hive bodies and listened, but he heard nothing. The frozen ground in front of the hives was strewn with dead bees.

They walked across the ice to the snake islands. The surface of the ice was crazed by deep cracks; it had made a map of its own faults. A strong wind flowed over the ice and took the place of the currents. Catherine's frock stood out behind her like a flag, and tears came to everyone's eyes.

At the island apiary, Thayer listened and heard the bees moving in their hives. He probed the dead bees away from one of the hive entrances with a stick. A few guard bees peered out. Everyone was glad to see them. There is a kind of faith which all animals must keep to survive the winter, even bees. At the bottom of this faith is the contemplation of life swelling up out of the ground again, so that all the loving and fighting can start once more, all the serenity, all the randiness and jealousy. And this expectation that spring will come is quite independent of any beauty and gentleness in the creature which does the expecting. The rats that live in cities will have new litters, and vipers will hatch from eggs as delicate as those of robins, because the promise of coming alive again belongs to everyone.

"I don't see why you shouldn't hope for the best," Thayer said. "They aren't dead yet, by any means."

90

"They don't *look* sick," Catherine said.

"But that may be deceptive, since it's apparently a disease of the brood, rather than the adult," Thayer told her. "You'll really have to wait until the queens start laying in the spring to see how things stand."

"I don't want to wait that long," McKay said. "What if they're sick in the spring, and we still don't know what it is?"

Thayer knocked the ashes out of his pipe. "I don't know what it is," he said. "I tried isolating some of my hives. They all became infected eventually."

"I've made up my mind to go and see him," McKay said.

"Who?" Catherine asked.

"Langstroth," McKay said. "The alternative is to give up."

"Well, let's not do *that,*" she said.

It was decided that an expedition to Massachusetts should leave in March. Sewall, McKay, and Colin were to go.

In contemplating Colin's departure, Catherine found herself contemplating his death. She imagined the experience of discovering him dead. The Crow would bring him back from Massachusetts on one of their idiotic sledges, covered by a blanket. She would approach the sledge without speaking, certain of what was there. The Crow would watch her. The blanket would reek of grease. As she pulled the blanket back, she would see dried blood still lingering at the corners of Colin's mouth. No one had wiped his face!

She imagined hundreds of places and times when he might die. Some of them were in the past. Once he lay dead beside her in the crib. A snake had crawled out from under the house and bitten him between the legs.

The evening before his departure, Colin skated with Catherine on the river. Their rhythm took them for miles without stopping, as if a wind were blowing them, although in fact the air was still. When they stopped, it was dark. Catherine put her arms around her brother.

"Look up," she said. "Look at those lovely clouds. I wonder why it is that in the day the clouds are darker than the sky, but in the night they're lighter. When you look straight up, and they're moving ever so slowly, the way they are now, you have the feeling that you're toppling over, or that the sky is falling."

13

MRS. FINGER'S SON was only twenty-four when he met his end. He was a strong and attractive young man, but in his twenty-fifth year he let his mind wander and encountered a fatal accident.

This happened in April, when Sewall, McKay, and Colin had been gone about a month. Mrs. Finger's son had shot several rabbits, and his mother suggested that he bring one to Catherine. Its fur was a lovely winter-white.

"The skin is only damaged at the head. Would you like me to save the pelt when I clean it?" he asked her.

"I'll clean it," Catherine said.

He allowed an incredulous look to cross his face.

"You don't think I'm capable of cleaning a hare? Watch me, then," she said, and made a very good job of it.

"She cleaned the rabbit herself," Mrs. Finger's son told his mother. "She took the pelt off as nicely as if she'd done it all her life."

"All of which goes to prove," Mrs. Finger said, "that no one is all bad."

Mrs. Finger held a poor opinion of Catherine, as she would tell anyone who would listen. Mrs. Finger's son, however, had reached the age of value inversions, where good and evil seem perversely to have changed places. A moment before reaching this age, the moral scheme of things stands forward clearly for the first time in one's life, so that the innuendo of adults can at last be comprehended as clearly as plain talk. The very next moment, however, one sees that everything advertised as wisdom is actually hypocrisy when more fundamental tests are applied. At the same time, certain forms of sinfulness are revealed to be very sweet.

I want, he kept hearing himself say, something, but I don't know what it is. What did he want? A career as a concert violinist? The adventures of a Canadian fur trapper? The power of a railroad president? A kind of raw potential seemed to rattle in his pockets like silver, and he would be damned if he would spend it the way his father had, putting music boxes into brass eggs. Sometime in the future, he would live in a large house by a broad river, and his wife and children would live there with him at a kind of still point, but between that day and the present, he found himself with time on his hands.

He decided to give some of that time to Catherine. His parents had favored him with white teeth, a strong back, and twelve years of violin instruction. In the years since his voice had changed, men and women seemed to want something from him, and as they could not tell him what it was, he gave them concerts on his violin. He did this now for Catherine, playing Mozart and Beethoven mostly, but occasionally Schumann when the solitude and intimacy of the moment permitted. He played for her in the salon of the hotel while the cold spring rain was falling and no one felt like going outside. She stood at a window and watched the rain on the river. Her yellow hair, the lovely push of her breasts against her clothes, and even her melancholy enchanted him. He wondered what her grief was.

She never spoke of it. Something was sapping her strength, blanching her skin, dulling her eyes, and she never said what it was. He assumed at first that it was McKay's absence, but certain of her chance remarks convinced him otherwise. It was something more. He entertained her, and this entertainment was very much the sort one provides for a convalescent— music, cards, distractions. Sometimes she fell asleep while he played for her, exhausted by something quite unseen.

In May, with the arrival of pleasant weather, they walked together to the waterfall and climbed the green hills across the river. Catherine allowed a casual liaison to begin between them. They left the hotel at different times to avoid notice. On the forest floor, in patches of light moving like underwater waves on the bed of a lake, Catherine allowed her mouth to be kissed and her laces to be undone. Mrs. Finger's son couldn't believe his good fortune, and expected it to end at any moment. Catherine's yellow hair glittered among the dead leaves. She closed her eyes tightly, but she never stopped him, she never denied him any new permission.

Mrs. Finger grew suspicious. She became even more suspicious when her son abruptly assumed responsibility for washing his own clothes.

He was embarrassed by this necessity, but decided that none of what was presently happening to him was his mother's business. He had strayed into a lucky cloud, and imagined that he was invisible to the world. Did the world want him to make pleasant conversation, save his money, polish his shoes? He would do all these things if the world would otherwise leave him alone. People around him seemed not to notice the change of season, but his own biology had suddenly become as messy as that of the plants of the forest. The corollas of the May flowers had spread open, and now their stigmas waved about, lewdly coated with thick secretions. The pollen which fell in showers from the pines would adhere to them and attempt a kind of sodomy, but success would be reserved for pollen of the same species, which would germinate, swell, and then penetrate the tissue of the stigma and enter the ovary. In the forest, maple twigs could not be bruised in this season, in fact could barely be touched, without causing the sweet sap to ejaculate into the air.

He lavished a patient devotion on Catherine. He built a house of sticks in the forest, with a sod roof tight against the rain. He transplanted flowers to make a garden around its door. The bed where they played was made of pine boughs covered with soft animal furs. When he undressed her, he did it slowly and patiently, and hung her clothes on hangers he had stolen from his mother's room. When they lay on their fur bed, Catherine's clothes remained standing, and guarded the entrance.

Mrs. Finger's son felt he was getting to know her, and any time at all now he would actually please her. He reasoned that no one was holding a gun to her head. She needn't come to him if there wasn't something about his company she enjoyed. He thought about her all the time, and often hallucinated her presence when she wasn't there. This imaginary Catherine was somehow his own age and mated to him in a sacred way. He knew the wishes of the imaginary Catherine and could satisfy all of them effortlessly. The imaginary Catherine was perpetually nude, but never seemed to be conscious of her nudity. She worked beside him in the flower garden. He had a recurring dream in which the imaginary Catherine was contained within his body and could be taken out and put back by slitting his own abdomen, the way he slit the abdomens of rabbits.

But not everyone can stand the tedium of devotion, and Catherine proved to have less stamina than most. When he played the violin, when he presented her with flowers, when he shivered with anticipation as she arrived each time at the hut, she found Mrs. Finger's son amusing. Even so, he was not a man for her in the way that men are a challenge to women. There was no way for her to carry on with him the war between the sexes which is fundamental to sexual attractiveness. He would not treat her badly; he was innocent of everything including wit; his temper could not be made to rise up to provocations.

He carried no handkerchief. He admitted none of her faults. He did not know her at all.

It was a shame when Mrs. Finger's son lost his life. He was felling trees to be used in the locks Colin was constructing near the waterfall. He was working alone. The trees had to be cut close to the banks of the river in order to be floated to the building site.

A lodgepole pine standing in an oak thicket caught his attention. The river was so high that the roots of the pine were under water. He had to stand on the bent-over stems of oak bushes to swing his axe. No one in his right mind would have done this. The tree spun as it fell and struck him dead. His body lay in the water among the branches for several days. No one knew where he was. On the third day, as the sun rose to its greatest height, his abdomen filled with death gas and his body drifted out into the stream.

Catherine had washed her hair and was combing it dry. She sat on the front steps of the hotel. The air was warm and quiet. The bees were working in a linden nearby. On the porch, in the shade, were two wicker armchairs, one turned slightly toward the other. The armchairs seemed to be enjoying their privacy. They seemed to represent two people sitting together, even when they were empty. McKay had put the chairs there for Catherine and himself, and while they probably meant very little to him, for Catherine they were a proposition, the proposition that he and she should sit in these chairs and grow old together.

Behind the chairs, through an open window, one could see the mirrors of the dining room, and the repeating images of a glass pitcher filled with water.

"Don't look at yourself in the mirror," she had once complained to McKay as they passed through this dining room. "You look at yourself in every mirror we pass."

"You do it more than I do," McKay had said then.

Today, the chairs gave Catherine the willies. To escape them, she walked down to a point of land which intruded into the river. The flat water put the glare of the sun in her eyes. Some bees were here in the grass by the river's edge, drinking. They were her only companions, and yet there was nothing companionable in their presence. They drank, and flew away, and others came. Their lives were all work, all women's work—housekeeping and foraging. They spent their lives in domestic boredom.

There was something floating, and it came very slowly downstream. Heat rising from the islands where the snakes lived made the air appear a part of the liquid water. The floating object bounced in the distance, not on water waves but on heat waves. Catherine removed her shoes and lifted her skirts. She waded in the shallows and let a kind of cold oblivion grow at her feet. She wished to have absolutely nothing on her mind. It would be quite enough to stand here and watch the willow trees as they sweated river water into the air.

But in the corner of her eye, she saw the body coming closer, and now she turned and saw who it was. Mrs. Finger's son lay on his back and stared at the sky, as if he had found a way to swim without moving his arms and legs. Catherine held her skirts out of the water and waited for him to come by. He was taking his time. Some moments he proceeded down the river headfirst, other moments feet-first. Eventually his face drifted by Catherine's knees. His nose barely cleared the surface—it was ringed with maple pollen—and his eyes looked at her from under the water. In a terrible way he had never done before, he looked past her and hurried on.

The Germans found him before evening and pulled his body out of the river. His mother could not be comforted. She screamed and tore her hair. No one could understand why he had been taken. Everyone had been his friend. At dinner, there were tears in everyone's eyes. In the midst of so much open feeling, Catherine found that she could weep for him, too.

But when she was alone, this was impossible; she couldn't remember him. In the kitchen she heated water for a bath. The water flowed out of the kettle's spout like a hot root going down into the soil. She took off her clothes and sat in the bath. She soaped her long arms and her smooth neck. She would never have a loving husband the way plainer women had. Plain women had husbands who made them feel beautiful with their devoted touches, their friendship, their gratitude. The beauty of plain women was only in their imagination, but it was there certainly.

She slid down so that the warm water licked her back. Her hand discovered the mound, and lingered. She visualized Colin's head descending between her knees.

14

MEANWHILE, Gordon McKay and his companions discovered that a bilious mood was rising not only in Kansas but throughout the United States. They reached Pittsburgh in the second week of April, and, as Thayer had suggested, they stopped in McKeesport at the rooming house run by Harmon Blennerhasset and his crippled daughter, Bernadette. Blennerhasset was the publisher of a small bee newspaper called *Ohio Valley Beekeeping*. The house was a two-story wood frame structure with the white clapboard exterior, dormers, and attached barn typical of small Ohio Valley farms. It was the first warm day of spring. McKay's company had traveled nearly two weeks in constant rain.

"You're welcome here," Blennerhasset said, "and you may stay as long as you like. I have no doubt that my neighbors will howl when they discover you're from Kansas, but if you ask me, slavery has nothing to fear from Kansas or Kansans. If slavery were really in danger, there would be a great deal else in danger with it. I wouldn't hold my breath waiting for a war over slavery, not while the banks run the country."

Blennerhasset's daughter, Bernadette, was a small woman with fragile beauty in her face. Her lower limbs had been paralyzed as the result of an accident. She moved herself about in a cane chair to which had been attached the hickory wheels of a goat cart. She was the mistress of the rooming house and propelled herself by hand back and forth among its responsibilities. She kept a vegetable garden behind the house and did all the work for it lying on her stomach. She had recently given birth to a child. No one knew who the father was, or even asked, since Bernadette made the question unwelcome. The child was simply hers, not anyone else's at all.

On the day following their arrival, Colin stayed in bed with a fever. Bernadette brought him broth, balancing it in her lap as she propelled herself in the chair. She moved about the house gracefully and quickly, and never struck anything, although she customarily rolled faster than most people walk. She knew how to brake with one hand and thrust with the other in just the right proportion to carry herself around corners, through doorways, over carpets, down long hallways.

Sewall and McKay had gone off with Blennerhasset to look at his hives. Colin lay in a sweat, and the house was quiet except when Bernadette passed. She made a sound like a single roller skate. Bedding or pillows or other household cargo was always piled on her lap. He watched her in the kitchen through his open door. The fever caused him to swoon in and out of sleep, so that most of the day he dreamed the incoherent dreams of sick people, but toward the middle of the afternoon he woke long enough to see Bernadette feeding her baby at the breast. The dusty light fell on her bare shoulders. As the infant sucked, it also vocalized, making the strange bird sounds of an Eastern language. The other breast hung ready, its brown nipple leaking milk. Bernadette's face was hidden by her red hair, which hung forward in great disorganized curves.

In the next two days, as he recovered, Colin looked for an opportunity to get her attention, but none came. He sat on an ancient velvet sofa in the parlor and turned through past issues of *Ohio Valley Beekeeping*. When Bernadette came through the parlor, she gave one-word answers to his questions. She refused his offers of help with the household work.

With the exception of his sister, Colin had never encountered a person who kept to herself so comfortably. He was deeply intrigued. There were labyrinths inside Bernadette that he wished to explore. He watched her in the barns, where remarkable labor-saving devices allowed her to do the farm work. All the hens could be fed by pulling a single lever—the grain came down chutes of tinned steel with the sound of rain. Water came to the hens automatically through pipes under the floor fed by a giant cistern. The eggs rolled over wire screens to a central collection point. Paths to and from the barns and among the various animal stations were boardwalks, so that in wet weather Bernadette's wheels rumbled haughtily above the mud.

"She designed all that herself," Blennerhasset told Colin. "She drew the plans for it all, and made the measurements, and hired old Ralph Baily to build it for her. He's one of our local ne'er-do-wells. No one thought he could stay sober long enough to take his tools out of his box, but Bernadette held him to his agreement. She watched every move he made, and had him to do it over again if it wasn't right. Then, at the end of the day, she fed him supper and drank whiskey with him until he went home."

Colin wondered what Bernadette's impression of him might be. There were only the faintest clues. She treated him as evenly as she treated Sewall and McKay, and yet there was enough of a difference, perhaps in the way she bantered and made small talk with the others but never with him, to suggest that she had marked him out separately. He waited for a signal from her. Each of them was weary of solitude and willing now to break it.

It came toward the end of the visit. Bernadette had her own hives of bees, at the end of one of her boardwalks, just beyond the barn. She asked Colin to help her carry some equipment as she visited them. The bees were contained in hives built up of many shallow supers, each only four inches deep. Bernadette explained that this was special equipment she had ordered made for her in a local mill. The shallow supers remained light enough, even when they were full of honey, for her to lift them off the hives. As Colin watched, she went through each of the hives killing the queen cells. The bees flew around her, and alighted on her lap, and crawled on the spokes of her wheels, but none of them stung her.

"I love to see the babies hatching," she said to Colin. "Look at this. Here's one just coming out. She's pecking the wax capping off."

"Where?"

"Right here," Bernadette said. She held the frame up with one hand and pointed with the other. "See, she's just coming through."

"How do you know it's a she?"

"Because she's coming out of a worker cell. The drones come out of drone cells."

Colin stood behind her chair and looked over her shoulder. Beyond Bernadette's knees stretched the prospect of the farm, which was far poorer and more dilapidated in this view than in the view from the road. Part of the barn roof was collapsed. A hayrake with no wheels lay abandoned in a field. The day was very bright. Bernadette's hair glistened like a red wound.

"They're so blond and fuzzy when they're young," Bernadette said. "That's the way they are when they're house bees. Later, when they're field bees, the sun darkens them. The hair on their abdomen falls off, or perhaps it gets rubbed off against the flowers."

"What do you do with all your honey?" Colin asked.

"I sell it."

"And what do you do with all your money?"

She smiled. "I save it," she said. "There's a certain thing I want, and the bees are getting it for me."

"Is it a secret?"

"It's not really a secret," she said. "I haven't told anybody about it, but that's mostly because it's no one's business but mine. Still, if you want to know, I'll tell you. I want to buy a little car that moves up stairs under steam power. It's built by a firm in New York. Harmon carries advertisements for it all the time in his magazine. It's made for invalids."

"Who's an invalid? I can't think of you as an invalid."

"I am, though. I can't get up the stairs. I haven't seen the upstairs of our house in three years. Harmon used to take me up on his back sometimes, but now he's too old to carry me."

Colin turned to look at the farmhouse. The clapboards on this side were rotten and falling away. Apparently Blennerhasset only painted the front of his house. Curtains were drawn over the windows of the upstairs rooms.

"As it is now, we hire a local girl to come in and clean the upstairs rooms after the guests. If I could get up the stairs, we wouldn't have to do that. And I'd like to be able to go up when I want to. My room used to be that one, with the violet curtains. I'd like to be able to go up there again."

Bernadette finished her work and closed the hives. She wiped the honey from her hands with a linen handkerchief.

"I was thinking," Colin said, "that it would give me pleasure to take you up there, if you would permit it. I haven't had a proper tour of the place."

104

She turned her green eyes upon him. "If you like," she said.

When they were back inside the house, Bernadette put away her hive tools and veil. She washed her hands and looked in on her sleeping baby. Then she rolled her chair to the foot of the stairs and allowed Colin to pick her up in his arms. He passed one arm under her knees and one arm behind her back and lifted her out of the chair.

"I'm very heavy," she said. "Don't do yourself an injury."

"You are not. You're quite light."

He carried her up the steps, past flowering wallpaper. Every tread creaked under his boots. Bernadette's feet swung like pendants. Her legs were thin. When they reached the top of the staircase, she indicated the room with the violet curtains. They went in. She surveyed the furniture, the bed, the dressing table with its mirror, the hooked rug, the dolls on the window-sill. "It's dirty," she said.

Minutes passed. She seemed powerfully distracted by the sight of the room. Colin put her in a chair.

"When my mother and I first came here," she said, "we never thought we would see Harmon again. He was in jail, we didn't know where, and my mother never spoke of him. My mother kept the hens, and I helped her, and we sold the eggs, and when we could afford to, we invited the minister to supper.

"When I was twenty years old, in the winter, my mother said she had a headache and went to bed. During the night, a terrible fever came over her. She screamed and cursed God and said that Harmon was her uncle. She had married her uncle and had a baby by him, and the sin of it was taking her to hell. I'm certain she was delirious when she said all this, but Harmon has never specifically denied it. He refuses to speak of her.

"That night, she walked up and down the stairs and all around the house, dragging a cape of blankets, and saying terrible things. I pleaded with her to go to bed, but she paid me no attention, and she died as the sun was coming up.

"I lived here alone through the winter, and in the spring I planted the corn myself. This was a happy time for me. I was getting to know myself thoroughly. It was as if another person had moved in to take my mother's place, and that other person was me. I put a new roof on the house, to save it from falling down, and that is something my mother never would have done. I tore down the rain gutters and replaced them with new ones. I painted the front of the house. I felt capable of anything. In May, Harmon knocked at the front door. At first, I didn't believe he was my father. He seemed improbably short. My mother had been a tall woman, and I didn't see, just mechanically, how they could have gotten together. I kept thinking that he would have had to stand on a chair to kiss her. From the day he arrived, he began with the bees. He had read about them in jail. Then he bought a printing press and started the magazine. He was always very kind to me, and he never ordered me about. I began to love him then, and I still do."

Bernadette turned her head toward the windows. They were full of a bright glare, but under the trees, in patches on the lawn, was a shade deep enough to keep the last remnants of the winter's snow, and here it was, in thin plates and crusts.

"Harmon shot me by accident," she said, "down there, just beyond those trees. The bullet went in my spine. He thought I was a fox."

This had happened in August, only four months after Blennerhasset's release from jail. He had been weeding the vegetable garden. His thoughts were on prison, and his wife's death. Each time he stooped to pull a weed, the blood rushed to his face, exactly the way it does when a man's mood freshens to a rage. His years in prison had softened his hands and weak-

106

ened his back, so that any farm work exhausted him now in a short time. He stopped often to look out on the horizon. The shagbark hickories, the cottonwoods, the isolated walnuts along the borders of his neighbors' fields stood still in the heat, every leaf.

But then he saw the berry bushes behind the henhouse move, and fall silent, and move again. A fox had recently been molesting the hens. The animal apparently had now grown bold enough to come in the daytime. Blennerhasset put down his hoe and crawled out of the garden on his hands and knees. He held his breath until he reached the barn door. His Sharp's rifle rested against an inside wall. He loaded it, his breath moving in and out in harsh tides. A cow and two chickens watched him at his work. When he was finished, he tightened the rifle's strap and slung it on his back. He returned to the garden the same way he had come.

Someone was burning a field on a distant farm, and the smoke rose as a perfect vertical column. Blennerhasset lay on his stomach among the cornstalks. Bernadette worked among the bushes, filling her pail with raspberries. The sun made perspiration stand out on her forehead.

Bernadette said, "Oh," when he shot her, as if she had just remembered something.

15

McKay's party reached Buffalo in the last week of April and secured passage for Albany immediately on a packet of the Erie Canal Navigation Company, the *Oneida Chief.* A vast program of renovation and enlargement of the canal was just beginning. The Erie and its branches—the Chemung Canal south through the Finger Lakes, the Oswego from Syracuse north to Lake Ontario, the Black River Canal to the Adirondacks, the Chenango Canal south to Binghamton—all these were part of a great system of inland navigation for the American continent, and they spread the cholera wherever they went.

The *Oneida Chief* left Buffalo on the evening of April twenty-fifth in light snow. On either side of the locks at Buffalo, the granite factory buildings and warehouses rose up. The water in the canal was only four feet deep, but the snow and the darkness made it appear bottomless. After her team drew her ahead into the first set of locks, and when the enormous doors had closed, the water was let out and the *Oneida Chief* descended like a bucket being let down into a well. Two mules hitched to the line boat behind the *Oneida Chief* watched her going down in the lock, their faces illuminated by gas lamps near the locktenders' shanty. One of these mules was suffering a complaint of the gut: its bowels ran and it farted constantly.

By nightfall, the *Oneida Chief* was running through the thirty-foot-deep cut west of Lockport. It was like being in a tunnel with no top. Colin watched from the deck as the sky cleared and the moon illuminated the outlines of clouds. The only deck space was on the roof of the cabin, reached by a small stairway at the stern. It required some innovation to make oneself comfortable on this curved surface, and he finally settled in a half-recumbent position, using a rung of the railing as a headrest. The navigation lights of approaching boats were pleasant to see. Once through the deep cut, low wooden bridges came up every mile or so. They were carelessly made, fastened together with long steel bolts. Colin saw great gaps of sky between the boards as the boat passed under them. Fresh snow lay on them to a depth of half an inch. He watched the mules swaying from foot to foot on the towpath for the best part of an hour before he returned to the cabin.

It had suffered a disagreeable transformation in his absence. The interior had been pleasant enough when he left to go above deck. It had been lined with cushioned benches under the windows, and long tables had stood in the center. At one end were a writing desk, inkstand, and modest library. Murals of New York State landscapes hung above the windows. But now the benches had been folded out into beds, and above them hung two tiers of sacking-bottomed frames for sleeping. A temporary screen had been hung up to separate the women passengers from the men. The tables were crowded with carpet bags, underwear, boots, shoes, food scraps, walking sticks, portmanteaus, and motley pairs of trousers. With some apologies and not a little difficulty, Colin gained the third-tier compartment which had been left to him, but here the human heat and the stench from so many open pairs of boots was scarcely bearable.

Near midnight, one of the women passengers was still reading by the light of a lamp. Her silhouette was thrown against the cloth screen separating the women's compartment from the men's. As the boat rolled and bumped the edge of the towpath, her head and neck moved ever so subtly and gracefully—more proof that balance and posture, along with the other determinants of sexual attractiveness, are below the level of consciousness. The lamplight put her form on the screen like a cameo, but she was a cameo who could turn pages. Once, when she turned her head a certain way, Colin was reminded of Bernadette strongly enough to feel the shock of recognition.

Finally she closed the book and began removing her clothes. She unbuttoned her frock, folded it carefully, and stowed it in her case. The man on the shelf next to Colin, who had apparently been sleeping, now sat upright. Other male passengers turned their heads toward the screen. The young woman opened her corset and took it off. She removed her stockings and stepped out of her garter belt. The garter belt required some bullying before it would move over her pelvis. She pulled her undershift over her head. She was now nude. The men in the cabin collectively held their breath as she searched in her case for her nightgown.

"Everyone mistakes my feelings," Bernadette had said once.

"I don't," Colin had told her.

"Yes, you do. Everyone does. You're especially considerate of me. People think I'm locked up in some kind of inner desperation, but I'm not. I like to be alone. I'm capable of more

alone than most people are with all their friends helping them."

"I know that very well," he had said. *"I'm considerate of you because I'm fascinated by you. You're very remarkable and good."*

The *Oneida Chief* stopped for provisions in Rochester. Here Colin left the boat and went on an errand. He found the Rochester Traction Engine Company, manufacturers of the Rochester Funicular Invalid Railway, on Genesee Street, two blocks north of the Erie. It was a large factory built of Medina sandstone with wire-reinforced glass in the windows. The stacks above the foundry rose sixty feet and let out smoke the color of ditchwater. Shore birds from Lake Ontario soared in the dirty plumes.

"I'll show it to you, but you won't like it," a man called Irish told him. "I wouldn't let any invalid of mine ride in it." Irish led him across the factory floor where people of all ages, even children, were working. The children were painting lacquer on the wooden parts for stationary engines.

The invalid railway operations were extremely modest by comparison with the activity of the rest of the factory. There were, in fact, no employees at all working on this part of the floor. A single demonstration model of the Rochester Funicular Invalid Railway was available for inspection. Its passenger car, on steel tracks running up a simulated staircase, was drawn by a cable which ran through a pulley at the head of the stairs and back down to the steam traction engine on the ground level. Irish explained how to light the boiler, which was fired by illuminating gas.

"One of the little disadvantages," Irish said, "is that it takes twenty minutes to get the steam up. You get plenty of time to change your mind about going upstairs. You'd have to be a fairly determined invalid, I'd think, to want one of these."

111

"In fact, I'm not that patient," Colin said. "Perhaps you could simply tell me how it works."

"I can tell you how it's *supposed* to work. You get in, give this flywheel a little start, and open the throttle. When you get to the top, you're supposed to close the throttle by pushing that lever up there. Half the time, it stalls midway between, and you have to get someone to come and start the engine for you."

"I've seen enough," Colin said. "Thanks for your trouble."

"It wasn't any trouble," Irish said. "I like to talk to people. I used to know everyone in this factory, but not any more. This place used to be filled with Paddys, all my friends, but Malley went mad with drink and killed his wife, and Sullivan drowned in the Ditch, and the bosses gave the rest of them the sack, so I'm the only Paddy left. And even in my case, I'm just a heap of tea in the bottom of the pot, and when I won't make tea any more, the bosses will scrape me out and throw me away.

"We all came to dig the Erie, and they said that when it was finished, we'd build our farms by the side of it. I dug between Rome and Lyons, through the swamp. We went through the Walton tract in the winter. The quarry men at Split Rock sent the limestone down to us on bob-sleighs, and barrels of salt to keep the concrete from freezing. They worked us at night in the light of bonfires. We tried everything we could think of to get thrown in jail, where at least you could sleep and be peaceful, but at the end of every day, more of us went to our graves than our beds. We put the bodies up on platforms with little roofs on them to keep the snow off, and there they stayed until a wagon was going to Rome, because no one wanted to be buried in the swamp. In the morning, you could see dog footprints under the platforms where the wolves had been jumping all night, trying to get the dead Paddys. When the wind blew hard enough to freeze the swamp, we lay in

112

the bunkhouses days at a time, naked together under the blankets to keep warm, and past caring with drink. Some of the boys fell in love, and let themselves be taken into damnation, because they expected to die, and they *did* die, but I lived, not because I was any hardier, but because I was touched by what is called the luck of the Irish."

There were geese swimming in the canal when Colin returned to it. Although a vast national debate was then current over the Erie, its costs and its prospects, these geese could not force themselves to be partisan for either side. As they floated here, German people, Scandinavians, Irish, and Poles floated by them. Everyone was going to the West, but no one was being sanitary about it. The boats were loaded so heavily that they scraped the bottom. Some of the immigrant boats had cholera and were not permitted to land. The immigrants took down their trousers and eliminated directly into the canal.

There happened to be no boats at all on the water this afternoon. The geese were the only vessels in sight. Colin sat on the grass of the berm and withdrew a pencil and notebook from a pocket of his jacket. He drew the plans for a funicular railway powered not by steam but by water. A hydraulic reservoir like a giant bucket would provide the traction for the car. Water would be added to this reservoir via a hand pump by the person desiring to ascend. When the reservoir weighed more than the car, it would slowly drop into a well, drawing the car upward. The direction of motion could be reversed by allowing a small quantity of water out of the reservoir. In Colin's mind, the car rode upward on noiseless wheels, pulling Bernadette in her chair with the absolutely certain power of gravity.

16

GOOD INTENTIONS and good works may be natural enemies, because they are almost never found in each other's company. With the best intentions, the Reverend L. L. Langstroth agreed to write a chapter for a New York publisher to be included in a scholarly book about bees. At the time he was solicited to do this work, it seemed a great opportunity. Among the other contributors was his friend Johann Dzierzon, the Silesian who was at this moment the elder statesman of beekeeping.

But despite the fact that the obligation was always on his mind, he could not begin to write. Always some other activity seemed to claim his attention—garden chores, or record keeping, or the part-time help he provided in his sister's general store. The publisher sent him letters asking where it was, and he wrote back long self-deprecating apologies with promises to deliver the chapter by a certain date. That date would come and go, without his ever approaching his writing desk, and eventually a new letter would come from New York. Even his friend Dzierzon wrote him once and pleaded for the work, but with no effect.

The publisher's tone became chilly. At last he wrote to say that Langstroth need not trouble about it any further; he had decided, over Dzierzon's objections, to send the book to press. Langstroth received this letter at two o'clock in the afternoon, and by three he had written the first pages of his chapter. He continued writing throughout the night. His sister's cat kept him company. In the weak lamplight, its pupils dilated to the size of a man's thumb. Langstroth kept a dish of fresh snow beside his desk, and rubbed his face in it from time to time. In the morning, the work was finished, and he sealed it up and carried it to the post office in Greenfield.

Two weeks passed in which there was no communication from the publisher, and then a letter arrived advising Langstroth that the editor had dispatched an assistant to visit him. They were unable to make any sense at all out of the manuscript, but were intrigued with one or two of the figures and were therefore willing to take the necessary pains to see the work into print.

The assistant turned out to be a young man with yellow hair and a sincere manner who had studied entomology under the great Agassiz at Harvard. Beginning with the first sentence and proceeding through the entire manuscript, he asked Langstroth first what he had written (for it was illegible), and second what he had meant. They sat together at the dining-room table for two solid days. Langstroth began this collaboration with as much cheer as he could muster, but he found himself exhausted before they had even begun to penetrate the manuscript. It was possible for him to read his own scrawling hand and therefore to say what he had written, but the meaning grew less clear the more he tried to think of it. The sense of the argument had disappeared for him, and he couldn't reconstruct it.

The editor's assistant saw that he was tired, and suggested that they work together for only an hour in the morning and then again in the afternoon, in order to allow Langstroth some rest. To his dismay, Langstroth excused himself from even these sessions after a few minutes, saying that he had to tend the garden, or feed the hens, or visit the bees. Finally he refused even to rise from his bed. The assistant sent him a note via his sister explaining that obligations in New York required him to return shortly. Langstroth apologized profusely, complaining of a ringing in his head, and asked the assistant to make his own sense out of the manuscript. This he did, by referring to Langstroth's research notebooks and by occasionally sending a written message to Langstroth asking for one bit of specific information or another. Langstroth was able to answer detailed questions about the outcome of long-past experiments or observations, and these answers could be verified by reference to his notebooks. In this, his memory was quite remarkable—he could repeat not only the protocol and results of past research activities, but also the complete text of shopping lists and notes to the milkman back through the past two years. He was in the habit of amusing his ten-year-old niece, who had just begun the study of Latin, by reciting the *Aeneid* to her from beginning to end, in three-hour sessions, all from memory.

When the assistant had finished writing out a revised version of the entire chapter, Langstroth read it and proclaimed that it was brilliant. Making a great show, he wrote a covering letter to the editor insisting that the young man be listed as co-author of the chapter. The assistant packed the manuscript away in his valise and shook hands all around. Langstroth's sister presented him with a pie to take on the coach. As they walked together to the coach stop, Langstroth put his arm around the young man and embraced him. He spoke in an animated, almost ecstatic way as they waited for the coach. He had a plan, he said, for a book in which the entire course of civilization would be traced out, like the plan of a river, or like the subtle branching pattern of a tree. From the tiniest feathery detail of the twigs to the powerful central current, it would be a Christian book, an historical book, a scientific book, and it would integrate subjects which were now thought to be disparate, only because they were currently studied by people who never spoke to each other. The young man said it sounded like an attractive idea, and promised to mention it to his editor. When the coach arrived, he was so pleased to get on it that he left his pie sitting on a bench in the waiting room. Langstroth discovered the pie, and ate it before walking home.

It was only a few days later that McKay's party reached Colrain, in a week when every farmer in central Massachusetts was preparing his seedbed. In some parts of Vermont, only ten miles to the north, so many farms had been abandoned by people going to the Western lands that the pine trees and the wolves were already moving back into cleared fields, but here no signs of this disintegration could be seen yet. One had a twenty-mile vista down the valley, of well-made farms, with every available square foot of black soil under cultivation, and only the woodlots on the slopes interrupting the furrows. When the horses stopped, it was possible to hear the bells of cows miles distant. These cows moved slowly over the green fields, crossing the veins of tiny streams, like white worms on a leaf.

Langstroth was in his bed on the day McKay's party arrived, and unable to leave it. His sister welcomed them into her house. She served them scones with their tea. There were several varieties of honey and jam on the tray.

"It's a pity you've come just as my brother's trouble has

117

returned," she said. "The worst of it is that I don't know how to advise you. You might stay for a few days and find that next week he has some relief and is able to speak to you. But I'm afraid that it's equally likely he will be in his bed for months. It's very awkward for me, and it always has been. I simply don't know what to tell people."

Langstroth's research notebooks still littered the room, and McKay asked for permission to peruse them. He found Langstroth's hand extremely difficult to read. Among the beekeeping records, Langstroth had written the drafts of sermons, the solutions to problems in Euclidean geometry, and lists of things to do. The letters in some words had been traced over many times, until they had grown too thick to decipher. Illustrations also crowded onto the pages—snatches of pastoral landscape; dimensioned drawings of hive designs; religious motifs; anatomical representations of ants, wasps, mosquitoes, beetles, bees; and human faces, hands, and bottoms.

"I think the old boy is lying, here," Sewall said to McKay when Langstroth's sister was out of the room.

"Where?"

"Just here, where he says he took sixty pounds of spring honey from a hive of what he calls his Italian bees."

"Why would he want to lie to himself?" McKay wanted to know. "These are his own notebooks."

McKay looked over Sewall's shoulder. "What the hell is that?" he said, pointing to an illustration.

"It's two bees copulating," Sewall said. "This one's the drone and this is the queen."

"Is that how they do it? How marvelous."

They found the Italian bees where the notebooks said they were, in a protected corner of Langstroth's apiary. The sight of these bees astounded them. At this time, the only honeybee found in North America was the European black bee, which had come with the colonists in the seventeenth century. Generally nervous in the open, frequently aggressive, reasonably industrious in behavior but subject to brood diseases and wax moths, the black bee had developed under the mild western European climate moderated by the ocean. For this reason, its brood production was not outstanding, and the springtime development of its colonies was tardy.

These bees that Langstroth described as Italians were somewhat smaller than the black bee. The color of the chitin on their slender abdomens was bright yellow on the sterna and the first four terga, producing bands of alternating black and yellow. The scutellum was also golden. Dzierzon had brought the first of these yellow bees from Venice to Germany in 1853, and already they were becoming the dominant European commercial bee. Because of their calmness on the combs, because of their unusually strong disposition to breeding, because of their industry and resistance to disease, Italian queens were at this moment transforming the stocks of apiaries throughout the world.

"Let's have a look at a queen," Sewall said. He opened one of the hives and removed a frame. It was heavy with bees on both sides. Only a dozen or so left the comb and flew up; the others remained peaceful. Sewall looked carefully through the comb and replaced it. He found the queen on the second frame he withdrew.

"Here she is," he said. He held the frame at arm's length, allowing the sun to shine through it. The workers surrounded their queen, each facing her, so that their bodies formed the pattern of a star, or explosion, with the queen at the center. Their attention appeared to be so entirely given to her that even their respiratory movements followed hers. Her long abdomen rose and fell, sending waves of breathing outward through the ranks of nurse bees.

"I've never seen such a beautiful animal," Sewall said.

119

But now McKay happened to look back at the house. At a window of the second floor, a man was watching them. A full head of white hair, dark clothes, the flash of spectacles. When he noticed McKay's attention upon him, Langstroth stepped into a shadow.

They took a room at the Colrain Inn, a massive red clapboard building with a leaking roof and a disagreeable bar on the first floor. At the invitation of Langstroth's sister, they joined her at her house for supper. They dined on cold venison and a pleasant sourdough bread.

"My brother suffers from a mysterious trouble of the head, a malady no physician has been able to cure," she told them. "It has prevented him from earning his living as a minister. He has twice been called to the pastorate of a distinguished church, and has twice had to resign when his health prevented him from discharging his obligations.

"For fully half the year he is himself, an engine of cheerfulness and good will. Then no project is too much for him. He completed the entire draft of his book, which you know is quite substantial, in a period of only four months. The farmers here have a short growing season, and in the spring they have to work with their plows and their cultivators from before dawn until well past dark in order to see their crops into the ground, but my brother works harder than they do when he is well, because he knows it is impossible for him to work at all when he is ill.

"When the illness arrives, it comes on rapidly, over a period of days, and takes him down into a despondency which must be something like the sadness which you and I feel from time to time, but he isn't only sad, he is utterly deprived of hope for no apparent reason. Nothing which gives him pleasure in health can give him any pleasure when he is ill. He has no wish to speak to anyone, and he rarely leaves his room. He forgets his passion for bees entirely, and behaves as if he were frightened of them. Even his enjoyment of reading is re-versed—he has only to encounter the letter 'b' in a word to suffer feelings he describes as remorse and terror.

"The physicians can find nothing in any examination which would explain the disease. They have tried the application of ice to his neck and the inhalation of salts, but these have never given him any relief. Once his head trouble seizes him, it takes him away from us for many months, as surely as if he had set off on an ocean passage."

17

IN THIS DECADE, Louis Agassiz served as the naturalist of the United States in the same way that Alexander von Humboldt had been the naturalist of Europe twenty years earlier. Each had been distinguished as a public man as well as a scientific man. Humboldt had been Councilor of State and Court Chamberlain to the King of Prussia; Agassiz eventually advised presidents and railroad barons. It had been a glorious age for zoology.

Agassiz had, in fact, been Humboldt's disciple in 1832, in Paris. The old naturalist had taken him to the Collège de France to hear Cuvier assassinate Geoffrey's doctrines of the living world. Agassiz had been unable to hear the lecture because Humboldt had persisted in whispering acid criticisms in his ear. Humboldt had coughed wretchedly and permitted himself to use his sleeve for a handkerchief. He would not have done this if he had been in the presence of an important person, but at this time Agassiz was unknown.

With Humboldt's assistance, Agassiz succeeded. Humboldt enjoyed discovering talent and educating it to the ways of achievement. He had provided advantages for the chemist Justus von Liebig and the mathematician Karl Friedrich Gauss; he now did the same for Agassiz. He counseled him on his choice of cigars and showed him an inoffensive method of breaking wind in company. He improved Agassiz's English, which at the time was poor. He passed judgment on Agassiz's women friends. He took Agassiz to dinner at excellent restaurants and even made him outright gifts of money.

Agassiz became a professor of natural history, first at Neuchâtel and then at Harvard, by following Humboldt's advice as conscientiously as a military officer follows handbooks. He was astounded to find that wealthy citizens were willing to underwrite the cost of his researches in natural history. In the company of nine Harvard undergraduates, two New York doctors, and the substantial Bostonians J. E. Cabot and R. H. Lyman, he navigated Lake Superior in a convoy of canoes, lecturing to his party as he went, and illustrating his discussions on a portable blackboard.

A major theme of these lectures, and the ones he gave throughout America in the 1840s, was the exposure of German *Naturphilosophie* for the lie and the heresy he judged it to be. Agassiz could find evidence in the fossil record that vertebrate fishes had existed in the oldest epochs. There was no possibility that a continuous development had taken place from lower to higher animals, since they had always existed together. The Bostonians were pleased to hear this. They were also pleased with the choice of wines, pleased to be drifting at the blue-green edge of Lake Superior, and pleased to be within the sight of savages but at the same time safely among agreeable company.

People always felt this way when Agassiz was speaking—that he was taking them on a perilous journey toward the origins of living things where they would be in great danger if they lost their guide, but of course they never did lose him. At the conclusion of one of his public lectures, they returned to their businesses and their politics on the same day they had left, with the sense of miles passed under their feet, and their Christian faith enhanced.

Agassiz published the scientific results of this exploration in *Lake Superior: Its Physical Character, Vegetation, and Animals,* a book which was well received both by the scientific community and the public at large. His zoological observations were supplemented by a pleasant account of the journey written by Cabot. Congratulations came from persons all over the world, including the English naturalist Charles Darwin, the Russian emperor Nicholas, and two whores in Scollay Square who had read the book aloud to each other between appointments.

Agassiz now found it necessary to revise his expectations upward every few months. His project to publish ten lavish volumes to be entitled *Contributions to the Natural History of the United States* enlisted subscriptions from every state in the union and every family of social prominence in Boston. At monthly meetings of the Saturday Club in the Parker House, he and James Russell Lowell, John Lothrop Motley, Judge Ebenezer Rockwood Hoar, and Cornelius Felton gazed at each other love-struck. He went fishing in the White Mountains with Emerson and Longfellow. They traveled at night to Laconia, pulled by a locomotive which shot live coals out of its smokestack on every power stroke, so that the wooden cars seemed in danger of exploding into fire. Because of his apprehension

124

of fire, Agassiz could not sleep on the train. The following afternoon, as he napped by the Pemigewasset, Longfellow put a live brook trout up his pantleg.

What is there about scandal which makes everyone feel that it strikes with poetic justice? It exists at every time in every place. All public men live in jeopardy of it, but only a few are stricken in any generation. Those few are cut down near the apex of their careers, as if scandal obeyed sporting laws and refused to afflict inconsequential men the way civilized hunters will refrain from shooting birds on the water. Agassiz was accused of improper relations with Jane, a young woman employed in his house. His accuser was one of his own assistants, a young Swiss who had accompanied him from Neuchâtel. There were other charges as well—Agassiz had published under his own name the results of the assistant's investigations in embryology; he had borrowed money and not repaid it; he had not compensated his staff for their labors in the past year.

A group of Agassiz's friends in Boston society suggested that a private tribunal be convened to evaluate the evidence for these charges. Depositions were taken. Jane was interviewed. Letters were solicited from bankers in Neuchâtel and Paris regarding Agassiz's financial affairs. The charges grew more specific—it was said that Jane was in the habit of going into Agassiz's room in the evening and staying until a late hour. He had given her gifts, including a gold watch. A witness had, on one occasion, surprised them together and noticed the front of M. Agassiz's trousers in disarray.

The tribunal decided in favor of Agassiz on each point, and the matter appeared to have been laid to rest. But a certain crankiness persisted about Agassiz after that, the crankiness of one who has only barely escaped ruin by scandal. Why me?, this person wonders. Why should I be singled out when everyone else does it and nobody says boo?

If Agassiz's social prestige suffered over the Jane business, his scientific prestige boomed ahead without interruption. Naturalists from all over the world sent the great Agassiz fishes and butterflies, and were paid for their contributions. More than once, Agassiz visited Thoreau at Walden. Together they bent over painted turtles. Agassiz was at that time quite heavy and could not keep up with Thoreau as he leapt through the trashy hardwoods. They disagreed over the age at which *Cistudo Blandingii* first copulates. Certain things Agassiz said caused Thoreau to wonder if he was on the level. "He thinks that the Esquimau dog is the only indigenous one in the United States," Thoreau wrote in his journal. "He tells his class that the intestinal worms in the mouse are not developed except in the stomach of the cat."

Part of the relationship between them had to do with the fact that Agassiz paid well and Thoreau needed the money. For the great *Contributions to the Natural History of the United States* Thoreau sent a shipment of fifteen pout, seventeen perch, thirteen shiners, five mud tortoises, eight bream, four dace, five painted tortoises, a black snake and a dormouse. The snake and the dormouse had come from Thoreau's cabin.

William Sewall was also a collector for Agassiz, but he had not been paid recently. Now, as it appeared that Langstroth had retreated for an indefinite period into his bedroom, Sewall decided to visit Agassiz in Cambridge and collect his accounts receivable.

He looked for him in Zoological Hall, a reasonable enough place to expect to find him, but he was not there. He spoke instead with one of Agassiz's disciples, H. J. Clark, a man whom Agassiz was training in his own image.

"I don't know where you'll find him, and I don't know what you can expect when you *do* find him," Clark said. "You won't get any money from him, I'm quite certain of that."

Clark spoke from behind a desk heaped with glass jars containing preserved fishes. The light from a nearby window flowed through these jars and produced odd rainbows on the wooden walls. The fishes themselves were outlined in color, like summer clouds.

"He's been fairly ugly since the Englishman's manuscript arrived. I wouldn't think of asking him for money today, even if I could find him, and he owes me plenty."

"What manuscript?" Sewall asked.

Clark searched under a pile of dried leaves and animal bones and withdrew a substantial sheaf of papers. "This one," he said.

The manuscript Agassiz's assistant now handed to Sewall was a preliminary draft of Charles Darwin's *Origin of Species*. Although Darwin had sent it to him with a note of explanation, and there was nothing in the note or the manuscript which could be construed by a reasonable person as an attack on Agassiz, the cloud of ink which Agassiz had let out upon seeing the book was secure evidence that it had struck some inner quick.

Sewall was also moved by it from the instant he opened it. The chapter titles, the list of illustrations, the first few paragraphs were as difficult to read as the books he occasionally attempted to read in dreams, because the ideas were his ideas, and yet they stood on a page he had not written. Here, in a flat and undistinguished prose style like the one a provincial civil servant might employ in his annual report to the London home office, Darwin assembled the evidence for transmutation of species, from his own observations and those of naturalists of all ages. As a Victorian scientist, Darwin's style was patient. Even his judgment of roses, and the relations of their varieties, was chaste and objective. But his thesis was radical, even incendiary. It burned Christian doctrine like trash.

"I would like to be left alone with this for a few hours," Sewall said, "and I am prepared to pay for the privilege."

"Don't be silly," Clark told him. "You're welcome to read it. I was just about to leave for home as you arrived, and now I'll be on my way. Pull the door closed behind you as you go; it locks by itself."

Sewall now fell into the substance of Darwin's observations. Darwin closed over him from above. He fell through the layers, and at each layer the greenness of the book increased, until its arguments were no longer arguments over specific grasses or finches or tortoises, but arguments over the greenness of every living thing, its sexual purpose, and its mortal nature. Some of this was threatening even to Sewall, who was not an entirely Godless man. When the machinery of the living world runs by itself, what is there for the Deity to do? Sewall himself had felt the presence, in the tropical forests of Caribbean islands, in the swamps of Louisiana, on the black plains of Kansas, during storms and droughts and infestations of insects, of something more than chaos as an organizing principle. A man is related to his God by prayer, but he is related to his mate only by fornication. When the prick is taut, the mind goes slack. And yet Darwin's suggestion was that the world is made better and more elaborate by its concupiscence, its randiness.

"Where is Clark?" a heavily accented voice demanded. This was Agassiz. He had come into Clark's office without knocking.

"I believe he's at home," Sewall said. "He left several hours ago."

"He's at home? He goes home in the middle of the afternoon? Does he think he works in a bank?"

Sewall introduced himself and explained the purpose of his visit.

"This Clark is somebody I have to get rid of before he drives me insane! Gratitude! I don't even *want* gratitude from him, although I've given him everything he could want to work well and money out of my own pocket besides. I suppose he

128

told you I'm a plagiarist. He did all the work on *Contributions,* and I signed my name to it. It's a wicked lie, but people are believing it! They will always believe the worst of what they hear. One day you wake up, and a vicious puppy you have raised from his mother's teat is saying bad things about you, and everybody believes him. Why do they believe him? Because his coat is so silky and his little bell jingles when he walks! This is how people decide who is truthful! It breaks my heart.

"You're an old fellow like me. We know what loyalty means! I sat through my youth at Humboldt's feet; this much is generally known. But at such a level you see more than people's faces, you see what goes on under tables and beds. I was discreet. I had information which could have embarrassed him seriously but I never told a soul. Today one would print what he knew in the newspapers, but then a young person was expected to keep his mouth shut."

With this, Agassiz turned to leave, but Sewall stopped him and raised the issue of his unpaid bill.

"See Alex," Agassiz told him as he hurried away. "He keeps the books."

Sewall searched through the building, and found rooms filled with snakeskins, whalebones, birds, turtle shells, strange rocks, dirty dishes, books, and heaps of laundry. He discovered Agassiz's son Alexander in an office in the basement.

"Papa has already spent all the money," Alexander said. "He hasn't paid anyone in five months. His creditors are filing suits against him in the courts. I would advise you to do the same, and get yourself a really nasty lawyer."

The following morning, a Saturday, began with rain, but by ten o'clock the crowd of people waiting in the streets around the Boston Courthouse was treated to a thinning of the overcast and finally to islands of open sky. Marshal Charles Devens and

129

his men brought their prisoner out into severe sunlight just before noon. This was the black man Anthony Burns, a runaway slave. President Pierce had sent a revenue cutter to take him back to Virginia. It waited for him at Long Wharf.

Because the abolitionists had tried several nights earlier to break into the courthouse and free him, Anthony Burns was now under heavy guard. Burns himself, however, was oblivious to both his jailers and his would-be rescuers, because his mind was blurred with art.

Two young women of the Society of Friends, Anne Bishop and Elizabeth White, had given Anthony Burns his clay. They had come into his cell and shown him how to work with it, how it must be kept not only moist but warm in order to flow smoothly, how it may be joined to itself by folding and massage. They had made the figures of animals for him, and he had copied these under their supervision, but when they were gone he no longer made the shapes of animals, he made the shapes of women. Under the encouragement of his thumbs, the clay swelled into the form of Elizabeth White's breasts. They hung within their network of ligaments in the superficial fascia, deep and globular, rounded by gravity like drops of milk. He created the nipples, erect landmarks above the pigmented areola with its little irregularities marking the areolar glands. He created Elizabeth White's thoracic cage, and felt the series of sternocostal attachments which descended between her breasts. He formed her abdomen and pelvis, and the fatty pubic mound lying over the pubic symphysis, which the real Elizabeth kept covered with hair. He created the labia majora and the pudendal cleft, and beneath the anterior labial commissure, the clitoris. If the clay stiffened and threatened to break, he warmed it with his lips. In the darkness of his cell, the clay and his flesh were the same color.

Anthony Burns kept his clay with him at every moment, in the pockets of his shirt and trousers, so that the clay would

130

stay at the same temperature as his body. He lived inside art the way a parasite lives inside its host and never comes out.

Now, although his mind was safely out of sight, his body was in plain view on the steps of the Boston Courthouse. Marshal Devens' men held his shackles like leashes. They walked him through the streets toward Long Wharf. The black man limped as he walked, favoring an old injury. The limp made him move like a trained bear past the carriages of the rich, who were watching the affair from within.

One of the carriages held Louis Agassiz and a party of his friends. This was not Agassiz's first view of a Negro. He had seen Negroes in the South and heard a great deal about them during his years in America, and had often been called upon to write and lecture on the relationship of the races as a zoological question. From his knowledge of the distinctions of animal forms, it was clear to him that whites and Negroes were possibly a single species, but that these two varieties of men had been created separately, obviously in different places, and certainly for different purposes. Now, as he beheld this black man, a revulsion came up in his stomach like the gas from a bad oyster. The pockets of the Negro's coat appeared to be stuffed with mud. This degraded and degenerate creature could almost be a trick upon us, he thought. God's idea of a joke, to make a beast in the form of a man.

Agassiz leaned back into his carriage, but not before Sewall had seen him. Sewall had been walking from his hotel, which was the old Griswold at the corner of Hanover and Clark streets. He followed Agassiz's carriage as it moved slowly through the traffic to Cambridge Street, and then up the side of Beacon Hill. Water was running down the streets, overflowing the open gutters. Drowned rats floated and skidded toward the Charles River. Green plants could be seen at the curved bay windows of town houses, and dull gas lamps lighting the expensive wallpaper. When the sun came through a hole in

131

the clouds, it provided a momentary light as bright as a photographer's flash.

The carriage stopped before a large yellow town house. Water was still draining from the slate roof of this building through vertical tile downspouts into the street. Agassiz's party walked through a garden heavy with the flowers of several species of the family Rosaceae—apples, cherries, peaches, roses, strawberries. The flowers of this family are ancient, even primitive.

A floral disk supports the flower parts, and it is this disk which, after fertilization, becomes responsible for the fruits characteristic of the family. In the rose, this disk is hollow and surrounds numerous pistils; in the strawberry, everything is reversed, so that instead of a hollow structure bearing the parts of the gynoecium, the carpels are borne on the outside of a raised disk. Sewall stopped to examine the strawberry flowers as he followed his quarry over the cobblestone path. These flowers were manfully attempting to hold globes of water as large as themselves. In this garden, each globe functioned as a separate lens for the sunlight.

Sewall straightened up and stood for a moment in the garden, enjoying the calm symmetry of the branches of the fruit trees. This was a rich man's garden, and the roses were a rich man's roses, but their beauty was a part of the natural beauty of the world, which is indifferent to the achievements of individuals. Although he was trespassing in this garden, in his present mood Sewall would have found trespassing a funny word. In his youth, Sewall had been entertained by radical ideas, but before he had gotten around to any acts of revolution he had found naturalism, and somehow naturalism made revolutionary acts unnecessary.

Nevertheless, it was now time to knock on Agassiz's door, and so Sewall strode up the steps. He knocked, and stated his business to a servant. In a moment, Agassiz appeared.

"Yes?" he said. Through the open door Sewall could see Agassiz's guests, in formal clothes, glasses of sherry in their hands. Close to the door, an attractive woman in a red satin dress was speaking to a gentleman with absolutely white hair.

"I want my money," Sewall told him.

Agassiz stepped onto the porch and closed the door behind him. He gazed into the garden as if he hadn't heard a word of this. The sun passed behind a cloud and seemed to turn off the colors of the flowers. Agassiz removed his handkerchief from his pocket and unfolded it. He dabbed at the corner of his mouth, then inspected the handkerchief.

"Is there anything on my face?"

"I don't see anything," Sewall told him.

"I thought I saw some pie crumbs on my face in the mirror a moment ago."

"I don't see anything now."

"Good," Agassiz said. "Now get out of here before I have you killed."

18

Now CATHERINE WROTE to say that all the bees were dead. Her letter came to McKay in the care of Langstroth's sister. The young Crow whom Sewall had trained as a beekeeper had become suspicious that the bees had been stolen, because they could not be seen around the hive entrances. He had opened the hives one by one and found them dead and stinking.

The news of death is such a clear violation of intuition that many people refuse to believe it. Wherever possible, people will insist on experimenting with the lifeless body themselves. They will stroke its hair, they will hold its hand, they will touch its face, and when these efforts at resuscitation fail, they will continue to be bewildered, and will weep on and on, not because they have acknowledged the loss, but because what has happened is out of register with common sense.

Bees are not human beings and are therefore not worth the same measure of grief, but the feelings which overcame Gordon McKay on the day after Catherine's letter arrived paid no attention to the proper proportions of mourning. A part of his distress was the distance which separated him from Kansas and therefore from the actual condition of his hives. It was possible that some of the workers and perhaps one of the queens were yet alive, deep in some moribund colony, and might be saved by skillful management applied immediately. If this were the case, Eli Thayer might be called upon to help. But Thayer had already admitted his helplessness against the disease. If he were capable of saving any bees, he would have saved his own.

McKay sat in a wicker chair on the porch of Langstroth's sister's house and looked at the orchards, the Berkshire hills, the cows and the church steeples. A vision of the hives dying came to his mind. In this vision, he imagined himself among the combs. As the bees expired, they lost their grip on the living cluster and fell through the black air, spinning, into the heap of corpses on the floor. Honey and excrement leaked down upon the dead and consolidated them into a cake. In McKay's mind, the bees falling between the combs had the appearance of people jumping from the windows of buildings into the street.

On this same day, William Sewall met a prostitute in the bar at the Colrain Inn and decided to take her to bed, although the clock above the whiskey bottles said it was only three in the afternoon. The whore, a middle-aged woman who served at tables in the inn, read a newspaper while she waited for Sewall to get an erection. As she was nearsighted, she put on her spectacles.

She was a heavy woman with long hair and white skin, and the sunlight scattered in all directions from her various proteins. Sewall watched her reading, nude, on the bed. Her legs

135

were apart. He was mildly put off by the sight of her vagina. It yawned open at him, its margins ragged, as if it had been formed by the bursting out of a projectile. This thought made it difficult to imagine putting anything in.

And, of course, Sewall was under the influence of his own specific melancholy. Darwin's book weighed upon his thoughts. The book was beautiful, but it was also monstrously unfair. It was unfair because, although Darwin's evidence was more complete, and his arguments were more sophisticated, his ideas were identically Sewall's ideas. Sewall had put these ideas to himself hundreds of times, and each time with more force than Darwin had cared to use anywhere in his book. But Sewall had never written them down, or even told anyone. And why? Because he himself was shocked by them. Yes, it's true that men and women spend their lives in pursuit of wealth and comfortable circumstances, and they allow themselves to be distorted in the process. Bankers are presumably not born greedy, nor are the poor already thieves as they lie in their cradles. But sooner or later, the changes come about, and they are permanent. One can expect to be as God made him only at the beginning of life, but he has a right to believe that he is fresh then. If the species themselves, like individuals, are subject to drift and compromise, then this last absolute cleanliness disappears. All absolutes disappear.

Sewall joined the woman on the bed and put his hand on her genitals. So this is the orifice in question. The hole that launched a thousand ships. It looks like a mouth, but it never smiles or says anything.

He looked at his own genitals, which were presently relaxing against the prostitute's knee. Although they had the opportunity of making a new acquaintance, they seemed resolved to mind their own business. The principal character was catching himself a nap between the testicles. Why are there two? Aristotle thought boys were sired from the right, girls from the

136

left. Sewall could not dispute him from any personal experience. Wherever pairs occur in the natural world, they are generally opposites. The members of these pairs will be superficially similar, but they will be one another's opposites in the functional, the essential respect, like positive and negative electricity. When males and females are young, they are all but indistinguishable, but sooner or later they get themselves jobs as adults. Only then do they have horns or breasts or whatever tools they think they need to do their work.

He closed his eyes for a moment and was instantly in the Cuban rain forest. The young Catholic woman lay back against the side of the mountain. A red-billed toucan watched her from a tree. Its beak was open, as if it were about to speak, but this was only its normal breathing posture. Its white chest rose and fell, its black feathers barely distinguishable among the shaded leaves. The blocks of ice packed on the burros' backs leaked water through their insulating jackets of mats and leaves, and this water dripped from the animals' abdomens. When the ice was gone, their work would be finished. In this way it served as a clock.

When Langstroth was told of the death of McKay's bees, he came out of seclusion to tell them what they must now do. They must return to Kansas and burn all the frames from every hive. They must scorch the interior wood of every hive box. They must scorch all their tools, and every piece of equipment which had ever been in contact with the bees. Only in this way could they be certain that the bacillus was killed. Every jar which had been used for the collection of honey, every piece of clothing that had been worn while working with the bees must be boiled. They must wash their own hands thoroughly before touching any bee equipment, once it had been disinfected.

Langstroth had given all these directions while descending

the stairs from his room. He came down wearing his clerical clothes, but these were as wrinkled as pajamas, presumably because he had been sleeping in them. At the foot of the stairs, he removed his spectacles and wiped them.

"I keep seeing spots," he said. "I thought the spots were on my spectacles, but they aren't. Sometimes they're as big as grasshoppers. Never mind."

His bedroom slippers skidded on the floor like snowshoes as he led them into the parlor. He sank down into a stuffed chair and buried his face in his hands. He remained this way for several long moments before he sat up and put his spectacles on again.

"I'm sorry," he said. "I've forgotten what we were talking about."

"You were telling us what to do about my bees," McKay said.

"You're the people from Kansas?"

"That's right," McKay said.

"I remember. I wrote you some letters."

"You did indeed," McKay said. "They were very encouraging."

Langstroth buttered a piece of cold toast and put it in his mouth. He stirred his tea, and drank most of the cupful in one long draft. "Well, I'm glad I was encouraging," he said. "I think ministers should be."

He looked out the window at the green fields and their parasites, the cows. The clock in the front hall struck the hour.

"What's the country like, in Kansas?"

"It's very nice," McKay said. "The eastern part of it is somewhat like this, with forests and hills. Toward the west, it turns into a flat prairie. Wild grasses grow there well. I should think it will all be planted in grain one day. And if you go farther west, you come to the mountains."

"I'm sold," Langstroth said. He put down his cup and saucer

138

on a side table. With a great lunge, he lifted himself out of his chair and shuffled out of the room.

McKay's party was naturally bewildered by this. They didn't know what to make of the situation. What had they done to offend him? McKay was distressed, Sewall was annoyed. Langstroth had apparently developed and abandoned an interest in their plight all in half an hour. Or so they thought.

Langstroth's sister came down the stairs, quite excited. "What did you say to him?" she wanted to know. "He's up there packing his trunk. He says he's going with you to Kansas. He says he's going to help fight the war against slavery."

"*We* didn't say anything about slavery," McKay said. "We were talking with him about bees."

"He thinks you're abolitionists. He wants to go with you to help make Kansas a free state."

"But that's not what we're trying to do," McKay said. "We're only trying to make a living and get rich if we can."

"Then you'd better explain that to him," Langstroth's sister said. "Because he hasn't got it at all clear in his mind."

But, as matters worked out, they never had an opportunity to explain it to him. Langstroth brought a miserable old trunk down from the attic and spent the morning filling it. He put very few clothes in the trunk, but loaded it instead with books and papers.

"Look at this, Margaretta," he said. "I found Michael's old house." This was a carved mouse house, imported from England. It was painted to look like an ancient half-timbered farmhouse. It had been given to Langstroth by his father in his youth.

"Are you going to take it with you?" his sister asked him.

"No," Langstroth said. "I don't think I will. It still smells bad. Michael peed in it once or twice."

Langstroth went up and down the stairs twenty times that morning, opening closets and removing their contents, looking under beds, asking his sister the whereabouts of something he could not find. At noon his sister made him a meal and took it to him in the barn, where he was looking through an enormous stack of letters. When he had finished the last letter, he announced it was time to leave.

Five hives of his Italian bees had their entrances screened up and were loaded on his sister's farm wagon. Langstroth's wretched trunk was put up beside them. He had found an old muzzle-loading rifle somewhere and put this in the wagon as well.

But in Greenfield, at the coach depot, Langstroth said he must return home to retrieve a book he had meant to bring. His sister's hired hand drove him away in the farm wagon, and returned several hours later with a note.

The note was from Langstroth's sister. She said that he had taken to his bed the moment he had returned, and was now so deep in melancholy he was unable to speak. On behalf of her brother, she apologized for the inconvenience, and urged them to accept the Italian bees as a gift to take to Kansas. Although he would not talk, her brother had passed her a message stating that this was his wish.

19

JOHN BROWN was now in Kansas, on the first of his three visits.
With his sons and a group of sixty accomplices from the Northern states, he was conducting a campaign of intimidation
against scattered slaveholders along the Marais des Cygnes.

Misanthropy and crankiness are widely associated with age.
Older people apparently have a right to their severe view of
the world, the way sugarcane has a right to its bitterness when
the sugar has been sucked out. John Brown had lost his patience
with Godlessness. When news came of the sack of Lawrence,
he put his sons to work sharpening axes.

No one knew why old Brown regarded the stories he read
in newspapers so seriously, so personally. When there is a railroad accident, when a bridge collapses, when sleeping children
are burned up in a fire, people will mention these things to

each other in barber shops and fish shops for days, but generally no one will attempt to do anything about it. There is this universal presumption that the event has come from God as a gift, like His air, like His light.

But occasionally someone will discover that he is more than the object of God's attention; he is also His agent. This person will see that he has an active role to play in God's affairs, and he will read news stories looking to see how he fits in. John Brown had made this discovery, and it had forced him to change all his plans. The news of the sack of Lawrence awakened peculiar feelings in his breast. His heart seemed to hurt. He discovered a lump in his throat the size of an olive. Feelings of disgust and impatience grew so strong in him they ruined his appetite and his sleep. He read over and over again the accounts of the timid surrender of the city and the pillage by the border ruffians.

When the axes and broadswords were sharp, John Brown loaded them into his wagon. His sons, Watson, Oliver, and Frederick, and his son-in-law Henry Thompson climbed in beside him. The old man and his sons! They were devoted to one another. The world was in schism but the family was intact! Before they left, Oliver remembered to slice a pumpkin for the cow's breakfast.

They drove toward Pottawatomie Creek, through a lovely prairie landscape interrupted here and there by running water. The wagon wheels divided brooks as they passed through. Rainwater ponds gave back the images of turning clouds. They saw buffalo grazing, but not their brutish faces, because the prairie grasses were already long.

Toward darkness, a heavy cloud of passenger pigeons flew over them and landed in the brush and slender trees beside a nameless brook. The weight of these birds bent the branches deeply, and broke a number of them. The birds fanned the air for balance on their delicate perches. They vocalized endlessly. Their feathers reflected the red light of the sun. It was as if a glacier had suddenly materialized among the trees.

John Brown and his sons camped here and built a fire. The birds stopped talking and put their heads under their wings. The old man brewed tea. Watson played his mouth organ. When darkness fell, they lighted torches and walked to the roosts of the sleeping birds. With little effort, they knocked dozens to the ground and butchered them as they lay stunned. If they had wished to, they might have filled their wagon with pigeon meat, but in fact, they were preoccupied with other business.

They cut out the birds' tongues and hearts, but otherwise neglected the carcasses. Old Brown prepared the meal in a skillet over the fire. Before he would allow his sons to eat, he sent them to the river to wash their hands and faces. The stupid pigeons who had survived the slaughter came to rest on the same roosts their dead brothers had left. While his sons were at the river, old Brown listened to the voices of the pigeons. Each of the birds was speaking to him, encouraging him, giving him instructions.

Toward midnight, he knocked on the door of the isolated prairie house where James Doyle lived. It was known that Doyle, a Missourian, had threatened the free-soil storekeeper at Dutch Henry's Crossing. When the door opened, Brown commanded James Doyle to surrender in the name of the Army of the North. He kicked the door open with his boot and found Doyle partially dressed. Doyle was naked from the waist down, having come only that moment from his wife's embrace. Doyle's sons William and Drury were also commanded to step outside. A younger son, John, was spared when his mother intervened with shrieks and sobs.

"Papa," Oliver asked, "are we going to kill this man without letting him put his pants on?"

Old Brown answered that question by raising his hackmore

over his head and cleaving James Doyle's skull in half. Then he drew water from the well and washed his tools before moving on to the next house.

News of the sack of Lawrence had also reached McKay's party, who were now making all speed back to Kansas. *The New York Times* had devoted headlines to the story for eleven days. Eyewitness accounts told of wholesale slaughter and depraved acts by the border ruffians. McKay had judged the urgency of reaching Kansas great enough to necessitate the expense of traveling by railroad. In Newark, they boarded the Great Pacific Line's *Western Horizon* for Pittsburgh and Cincinnati.

"I find rail travel very tiresome," Mrs. Ardmore said to Colin. Mrs. Ardmore was an Ohio farm wife returning home from a visit to the East. They sat side by side on a wicker bench between Harrisburg and Altoona. "The noise is terrible, the jogging back and forth is terrible, but I think I could stand all those things if I only had my privacy. It simply doesn't exist. Privacy doesn't exist in a railroad car.

"I don't understand why people can't mind their own business. If I look at my watch, someone will say it's disgraceful the way the train is late. If I tuck up my hair and roll back my sleeves, someone will say there's nothing like a good wash. I don't inflict myself on strangers and tell them my life story for the pleasure of it. Why do they do it to me? People snatch my privacy away as a matter of course, the way they remove matches from the hands of children. I don't understand why they think I oughtn't to have it. When did the possession of privacy ever kill anyone?"

In Pittsburgh there was an hour's stop. Colin left the train and found a shop that sold writing paper. He took the paper into the lobby of the station hotel and wrote a short letter to Bernadette, proposing marriage.

The interior of the station hotel was quite luxurious, with leather furniture and glass chandeliers. A young woman with yellow hair attended the registration desk. The polished floor gave back her reflection as accurately as the surface of a lake. When she stood up to answer someone's question, a portion of her hair fell out of its combs. Colin watched her put it back. She felt his eyes on her and turned away.

When Colin had posted his letter, he walked outdoors to the station concourse. It was raining. He visualized the letter making its way to Bernadette. It would be sorted, and put in a sack, and moved by rail, and sorted and sacked again, until it reached her.

He had written and posted the letter all in a quarter of an hour, without a moment's hesitation or reflection, but now he was overcome by feelings which deserved to be called second thoughts. By her own assertion, Bernadette was an invalid, and her life was full of restrictions. Colin did not know, and had no way of evaluating, how far these restrictions might extend. She said she had no feeling below the waist, but she had become pregnant and given birth to a child. Had she done this entirely as an experiment? It was possible. She knew the limits of her injury to a high precision, and she would have determined these limits by probing the boundaries. Had she taken a man into her bed the way she took a pin in her hand and stuck herself, the way Colin had seen her do, to see whether the margins of the numb region were moving? It was possible.

And, of course, he wouldn't want to be used this way.

He recalled her face and her voice very clearly, almost as if her real presence were next to him. He could do this because he loved her. Summoned up this way, from his imagination, she was always very sexually promising, and never in a mood for serious questions.

In an instant, he saw that he must return to McKeesport himself. He woke McKay and told him his plans.

145

20

COLIN MADE and revised his drawings of the hydraulic funicular in railway cars, in waiting rooms, and at the tables of the grim refreshment parlors where he took his meals. He visualized the geometry of the carriage and its rails in ten or twenty alternative configurations. He considered safety features, including a braking arrangement which would automatically stop the carriage if its speed became too great. All the fittings and hardware appeared in his mind. He made lists of material, and catalogued the tools that would be required for the work. Each design was an experiment which he had to judge successful or unsuccessful only after he had drawn it and thought about its characteristics. He began and completed the construction in his imagination so often that he seemed to have built hundreds of funiculars. He became experienced in the construction of funiculars, although the experience was entirely imaginary.

None of the designs satisfied him. There is an obligation which comes after an imaginative idea, an obligation to work out the details. Colin suffered under this obligation and wondered how the original pleasure of the conception could be disappearing merely because he was now considering the individual parts. He spent two days in Pittsburgh buying materials, and his pleasure decreased still further. The rail stock was unavailable and had to be replaced by iron pipes. The bearings for the car had to be machined specially and would require a return trip. The manufacture of the brakes would take still longer.

Each of these compromises seemed to threaten the entire possibility of the project. The funicular in Colin's mind could withstand an attack of four or five substitutions, but not fifty. A spring-loaded cable tensioner was not available; he must use turnbuckles instead. Colin felt the unfairness. Why is the world's supply of materials so poor when its supply of ideas is so rich?

He hired a freight wagon and drove to McKeesport along the Youghiogheny. Red birds of a species he didn't recognize started up from the corn. From the top of a gentle rise, he had a view of Blennerhasset's farm, more than a quarter of a mile away. He stopped the horses. In the quiet air, he could hear Bernadette's hens having an argument. Bernadette herself was outdoors. He saw her emerge from one of the outbuildings and move along the boardwalk into the henhouse.

He set the brake on the wagon and climbed down from the high seat. He walked to the river and looked into its reflections, but there is never any advice in the contemplation of pleasant scenery. People in difficulty have traditionally separated themselves from other people and looked into quiet ponds, seascapes, and mountain views for answers, but it is unlikely that anyone ever learned anything from a sunset. Colin had made up his mind to return to her, had in fact thought about little else since leaving her, but at this moment he felt like an intruder. The sight of Bernadette at her work made him doubt the wisdom of interrupting her. But what were the alternatives now? He could empty the freight wagon by the side of the road and return to Pittsburgh. No, he would go ahead.

Bernadette came out on the front porch to meet him as he drove into the farmyard. She held a cat on her lap. Her arms and her face were as white as the cat's fur. Her green eyes were iridescent. "What's all this?" she said.

Colin looked down from the wagon seat. "It's what we need," he said. "I'm going to make something nice for you."

He took off his hat and coat and put them on the seat beside him. His yellow hair rose up toward the sun like a gas flame. The coat was small enough for an adolescent boy. He stepped down and began removing the contents of the wagon. Both Bernadette's eyes and the cat's followed him.

"No one ever courted me with so many building materials before," she said, speaking to Colin's back. "Is this the way you do it in Kansas?"

He answered without turning around. "It's one of the ways," he said. He brought out the iron pipe, the cable, and the timber and made a pile of it by the front door.

There was an ambiguity in Bernadette's reception which left Colin wondering whether or not his letter had arrived. For the hundredth time he regretted the tone of the letter, its presumption, its insistence. Fully half of the text had been a set of directions for finding him in Kansas. He had written the letter from one practical person to another. Its substance was a direct offer, followed by a set of instructions for accepting the offer. But now he regretted the letter because it was im-

148

modest, because it was brash, because it was not from himself to Bernadette but from one grain merchant to another, and he resolved to intercept the letter if she had not already received it. He learned the time of the postal deliveries, and made himself useful by bringing the post in from the box.

The construction of the funicular went forward. The first project, and the most extensive structural task, was the installation of the well for the water-filled counterweight. Colin was aided here by the deep cellar excavation under the house. The counterweight itself was a wooden barrel with a capacity of fifty gallons. It was filled by a hand pump from above and drained into a dry well below. The hemp cable ran through a pulley at the head of the counterweight shaft, under the stair treads to another pulley beneath the second-floor landing, through a third pulley above the landing, and back down to its point of attachment on the car. The pipe rails for the car occupied half the width of the stairs, but did not prevent the normal use of the stairs by one person. Colin's small stature occasionally caused him difficulties, as for example when the counterweight tub had to be installed in its ways, but he ultimately succeeded in lifting the tub on a series of stages.

In the evenings, they sat together on the back porch. In this night view, the poverty of the farm was disguised. The silhouettes of the henhouses and the abandoned hayrake lay against the skyline. There were many fireflies.

"How tall are you?" Bernadette asked him on one occasion. He told her.

"I was an inch above that, the last time I stood up," she said. She was wearing a delicate lace shawl. Her frock was a red velvet pattern she had sewn several days earlier. Was she giving more attention to her dress? Yes, definitely. These were better clothes than the ones she had worn on his first visit. Then she had worn working dress throughout the day, and her face and hands had often shown the soil of the last task.

149

Now her long red hair was brushed, often braided, and although her chores required as much from her, she seemed less devoted to them.

"It's peculiar to think that if Harmon hadn't shot me, we'd have very little use for each other," she said, "because it looks so odd to see the woman taller than the man."

She opened her breast and suckled the baby. Its smacks and groans, as it held the nipple between its lips, sounded like a room full of lovers.

Bernadette was allowing herself to be courted, but she was doing this in such a deliberate way that Colin felt put off by the responsibility of being her suitor. She apparently had told Harmon to keep himself scarce. Whenever Colin and Harmon chanced to meet, the old man quickly excused himself and went in the opposite direction. As Bernadette's suitor, Colin found himself in an official capacity in the house. Neighbors and tradesmen who came to the door would know his name, and would ask after his progress, and although he assumed they were inquiring about the construction of the funicular, there was room for the interpretation that they wanted to know about his progress with Bernadette.

Each day Colin waited for this progress, and each day it was postponed. Bernadette prepared his meals and assigned him a permanent position at the kitchen table. The baby also had a place at the table—Bernadette made it their chaperon. She allowed it to function as the most severe of chaperons as she listened for its crying, even its breathing, and sometimes asked Colin to be quiet so she could hear it.

And yet she apparently expected him to do something, to make some argument, to advance some proposal, which he had neither the privacy nor the encouragement to accomplish. She put on her attractive clothes and took unusual trouble with the food, but these were the gestures she had taken in her youth to meet a minister or a tutor. She was allowing herself to be courted, but without any spontaneity or pleasure. She apparently did not know how courting was done.

For his part, Colin retreated. He spent the day with his tools and his construction, and when it was necessary he drove to Pittsburgh for additional supplies. He completed the rails and the traction apparatus, and began construction of the car. He worked in the barn, under the supervision of the milking cow. To establish its proportions, he made measurements of Bernadette's chair, but he did this at a time when she wasn't in it. He spent a great deal of time on the car, until it was almost as elaborate as the carriage of his original conception. Bernadette's chair would be secured to it by a sturdy locking mechanism.

Working with his saws and planes, Colin enjoyed the color and the smell of the spruce as he cut it. He considered how his situation was on the one hand satisfying and on the other bewildering. His satisfaction derived from the project, which was nearly finished. His bewilderment derived from the woman, whose feelings he had never seen quite transparently. Her present disposition allowed him to wonder whether he would ever see her feelings. And yet he admired her ardently, and was prepared to have her under almost any circumstances.

At the end of six days, he still had not intercepted his letter, and he thought for the first time that it might be lost.

When the funicular was finished, Colin rode it to the top of the stairs, and although the ascent was a trifling dozen or so feet, the sense of rising with no effort was exhilarating. The only sound which betrayed the machine's vertical progress came from the centrifugal weights of the speed governor, which made a faint whir like the clockwork of a music box. With the counterweight in balance, he found that as little as two cycles of the pump handle would provide sufficient force to carry the car to the top at a dignified speed. A similarly modest valving of water would allow it to glide back down. The car ascended or descended in accordance with the principle of buoyancy, a buoyancy which was always under the control of the operator. It was like a bubble rising from the bottom of a lake, but it was a bubble which was prepared to go back down again when commanded.

Bernadette was very pleased. On her first ascent, she brought her cleaning supplies with her and washed the upstairs windows.

"It has its own intelligence," she said when she came down. "Like a horse."

In the afternoon, Bernadette left the baby with the hired girl and took Colin out berrypicking. The wheels of her chair made a grumbling cart noise on the gravel road. They left the farm behind and followed the river until it turned away from the road. The oaks at the margins of Blennerhasset's fields were ostentatiously heavy with leaves, as if they were pretending that leaves were an agricultural crop. The yellow grasses in these fields were bright with reflected light.

Colin carried Bernadette over a stone fence into the berry field and put her down. She moved on her stomach between the patches, pulling herself forward on her arms. Her feet trailed behind like a rudder. The berries rained into her pail with a steady rhythm. Her head was barely above the daisies. Colin watched her from a distance, nearly hidden among the flowers, her red hair lifting from time to time into view like a careless tail, and he was shocked to remember how she had been injured.

Toward evening, they rested together in a patch of moss.

"Well," Bernadette began, "how would you say our courtship was going?"

"I hadn't thought about it," he said. This was a lie.

"Think about it," she said. "Not much is happening. What's the matter?"

The light on her face demonstrated its structure, favored its beauty. What's the matter? This question is always full of audacity. It's the shortest and most sober of questions, and yet it may not be given a short answer. You pay me too little attention, he might have said. You entertain me too little. You work me too hard. But this last would not be quite true.

"You seem happy enough alone," he told her.

"Come lie beside me," she said.

He did, and at her invitation, they shared a sweet kiss.

She pulled his head to her breast. "You're quite remarkable," she said. The sound of her voice came into his head through her chest. "You're generous, and thoughtful, and clever with your hands. And if you know that I'm happy alone, you know a lot. That makes you quite intelligent, to have discovered such an important thing about me. But in other ways, you're silly and slow."

She folded her arms around him. "When I first saw you, I thought, Yes, there's someone very nice, and I might give him more of me than I usually give to people. But since you've come this time, I've found our courtship very boring. I really wish you'd leave me alone to think about you. I'd like to be alone to think about you, without your actually being here."

The following morning, as Blennerhasset drove him to Pittsburgh, Colin asked him to be on the alert for the letter, and to destroy it if it should ever show up in the post.

"That letter," Blennerhasset told him, "arrived before you did. She's had it all the time you were here."

21

THE STEAM VESSEL *Natchez,* on which McKay, Sewall, Edward, and Jiffy had traveled from Cincinnati, was commanded to stop near Leavenworth. The border ruffians had posted a field battery on the river, commanding the passage. Their executive officer was General David Atchison, who was at one time a U.S. senator from the State of Missouri. Immediately upon coming aboard, General Atchison kissed several women and helped himself to the captain's whiskey stores. But before much substantive searching could be accomplished, one of the border ruffians discovered the hives and a panic spread through the ranks. The Missourians quickly excused themselves and made for shore. General Atchison said terrible things to them as they were leaving, but finally went along himself. Before he left the boat, he disappeared for a moment into the galley and stole a pie.

They found Lawrence extensively ruined. Many houses had been burned to the ground, so that all that remained was a cellar hole and a chimney. The Missourians who now occupied the city called these blackened chimneys "Buford monuments" after their chief. And the city was being taken to pieces and transported east into Missouri. McKay's party passed a large group of Missourians who were attempting to remove the gilded weathercock from a church steeple. They were firing shotguns at its wooden supports. Their stray charges occasionally struck the cock itself, which spun like a gyro in its torment.

"It's all getting very nasty," Genevieve Thayer said when they arrived at her house. "Yesterday morning, I saw a woman in my garden pulling up the vegetables. Well now, at this time of year, the carrots are like little bitty pieces of string, and the onions wouldn't hide your thumbnail. She was even taking my melons, and there wasn't a one bigger than a pickle. I went out and spoke to her, and she said the troops were paying her to take everything out of the gardens. She said she was only doing her job. Can you imagine that? I've seen some casseroles bigger than the whole harvest she took out of my garden, and she got every last thing."

"Where's Eli?" McKay asked.

"He's still hiding," she said. "He hides in different places on different days. I don't know where he is today."

"We brought him something," McKay said. "We brought all of you something, as a matter of fact, but his present is the best."

"Oh, dear," Genevieve said. "I hope it isn't a gun. People keep giving him guns and he keeps losing them. I don't think he'd know what to do with a gun even if he could remember where he'd left it. Guns are always going off around here, and I'm frankly sick of listening to them."

"It isn't a gun," Sewall told her. "It's a hat."

They brought it out and showed it to her. It was a high silk stovepipe with a narrow brim.

"That's very nice," Genevieve said. "It's very elegant."

"It's the best Boston can do," McKay said. "We told the man it was for a mayor, and this was what he thought."

"I like it," Genevieve said. "It was a good choice."

"Eli asked us to get it for him, actually," McKay said.

Genevieve's surprise for them was that Catherine was staying with her in Lawrence, helping to care for the baby. Catherine brought the baby down into the parlor and cradled it in her arms as she told them the news from their own settlement.

"I blame all of you, and especially McKay, for the state of things as they are now," she said. "Everyone knows that Germans need authority, and yet you left without putting anyone in charge. They kept asking me to appoint someone, but I know them all so vaguely I couldn't decide. If someone had been clearly in authority, we might have survived the fever much better than we did.

"In May, so many people were sick that the planting was never done. I kept looking into the fields and wondering why no one was there. The German who brings the milk said there was a very sick man in his cabin, and would I come and see what I thought of him. I don't know why he asked me, since I am in no way renowned as a nurse. I told him he would get as much medical skill from me as from a freshly caught Hottentot, but he persisted. I went with him to his cabin, but by the time we arrived the sick man was nearly dead. He was an old man with very gray hair. I had never seen him before. His mind was badly worn by the fever. He lay under a heap of buffaloes, and he kept saying, 'It's so hot, it's so hot.' I washed his face and fed him some broth, but all the time

156

he kept saying, 'It's so hot.' Finally I thought perhaps one of the buffaloes could be taken off, since he was so very uncomfortable. There were literally four or five buffaloes stacked on top of him, and remember, this was late spring. But the very moment I removed one of the buffaloes, he said, 'I'm so cold, I'm so terribly cold.' He died before it was time to feed him again."

In response to their questions, Catherine continued her account of recent events. Scandals and short supplies had left everyone, even those untouched by the fever, in short temper. The sales of "Old Dog Tray" music boxes in Missouri had been disappointing. The few crops which had been planted were being eaten by wild animals.

"Don't tell me any more," McKay said. "I don't want to hear any more just now. I think I need a little nap."

"Whatever you like," Catherine said. "Please yourself."

McKay and Sewall departed the next morning, but Catherine stayed on in Lawrence until Colin arrived the following week. On the evening of his arrival, Catherine persuaded her brother to take her out into the saloons. They had done this before, in Boston, when they were living together on Beacon Hill. She put on Colin's clothes, and gathered her hair under one of his hats, and wore his shoes, and otherwise altered her appearance to impersonate a man. In this way she had often passed for his companion.

Dressed in Colin's clothes, she felt more than amused by their resemblance—she felt deeply pleased, even dignified by it. They were brother and sister, but she might have been him; this was the proof of it. They were doing this for an amusement, but the sight in the mirror she had of herself now was the sight of a man. She was a man in every view, from the front, back, and side. There was only something about her cheeks and her eyes which gave her away. She saw that even

157

this flaw in the disguise was to her advantage—she might reveal herself to someone if it suited her.

They walked together under the silver maples which stood at the border of Eli Thayer's property. Somewhere dogs were fighting. Their snarls and barking stopped and began again in regular tides, like the breathing of a sleeper.

"Mother would have liked this place," Colin said.

"I can't imagine why."

"It's so flat. She always said that children need a flat place to play while they're growing up. She pitied people who tried to raise children on hills."

"I don't remember a thing about that," Catherine said.

"Oh, yes," Colin said. "Living in a flat place was quite important to her."

They came to a saloon, and took a table. Colin ordered beer for both of them. In a corner of the saloon, an old woman played a piano and sang in a cracked, falsetto voice:

> "I made a bird of pine pitch,
> And flew him in a tree.
> I taught him to love the truth for his own,
> And leave the lying to me."

This saloon was enjoying the patronage of a large number of persons, most of whom were apparently from Missouri. A Missourian would recognize another Missourian by asking if he were sound on the goose. No one knew quite why they asked each other this. Most of the persons at the bar were demonstrably sound on the goose. Over their heads one could see, in chinks between the cedar shakes which constituted the outside wall, the light from mischievous fires.

When Colin put his elbow on the table, causing it to move the smallest fraction of an inch, Catherine was surprised to discover that even this small motion brought a stir in her feelings. She had missed him so terribly! These past four months she had been aware of his absence, and very little else. She would be distracted by newspapers, distracted by her work with the accounts, distracted by sleep, but only distracted, never relieved. When she awoke, there would be a few moments of peaceful forgetfulness, but she would always find her grief soon enough, generally before breakfast, and her grief always seemed to be Colin's absence.

"As there is a lull, let me tell you something very pleasant which is happening to me," Colin said. "I've proposed marriage to a person in Pennsylvania."

Catherine was silent for several minutes. "A person?" she asked finally.

"Yes," Colin said. "A lady by the name of Bernadette Blennerhasset."

"Oh," she said. "That's extremely nice. I've heard they have pretty women in Pennsylvania."

"Yes," he said. "They do. I suppose there are pretty women everywhere, but Bernadette is in Pennsylvania."

"Well," Catherine said, "this *is* exciting. How did you find her? Did you pick her out of a catalogue? Genevieve showed me a catalogue of women who want to be wives. They tell all about themselves. They say what kind of man they want, and where they want to live, and you can write to them. I think it's very sensible. I mean, it doesn't leave it all to chance. You say what you want, and she says what she wants, and if they're the same, you take each other. If they're not, you leave it alone. No one has to marry the boy next door any more because he's the only pair of pants for twenty miles."

"I didn't find her in a catalogue," Colin said. "I found her in person."

"Well, then, all the better, as you know what you're getting. You aren't just answering an advertisement."

"She's crippled," Colin said. "Her legs don't work. She moves around in a rolling chair she made herself from the wheels

159

of a goat cart. She has a little child, though she has never been married. She keeps bees and runs a boardinghouse."

Catherine looked away. She remained silent for several minutes, listening to the old woman at the piano finish her song. The voices of the border ruffians at the bar made an even background, occasionally punctuated with an argument, the way the voices of hens in a fowlyard will sometimes rise up for a moment until a slight is punished and forgotten.

"I don't think you're very nice," she said, "to tease me about something so important."

"I'm in *earnest,*" Colin told her. "I'm *absolutely* in earnest."

Now the woman who had been playing the piano rose from her stool and made her way through the tables toward them. She lifted her skirt to clear the rather thick mud on the floor.

"May I join you?" she asked them. Her speaking voice turned out to be several octaves lower than her singing voice. She drew up a chair and sat down, smiling, and waited for them to recognize her.

"Eli Thayer!" Catherine said, after a delay.

"You guessed it," Thayer said, "but keep your voice down."

"What are you doing dressed like that?" Catherine asked him.

"I might ask you the same question," Thayer said, "but I won't. You have your reasons, and I have mine. Mine are fairly transparent, however. I'm hiding from the border ruffians."

"This is a silly place to hide from them," Catherine said. "They're all here."

"I'm not only hiding from them, I'm spying on them," he said. "They generally sit here and drink for hours before they make up their minds to go out and shoot somebody. In that time, I can provide some sort of alarm. Old General Buford gets so drunk, I worry about him falling off his horse. He spends most of his time in here. He's always kissing me and feeling inside my dress. He's a sad old fellow. How could anybody enjoy squeezing a titty made out of handkerchiefs?"

"I think I would like a whiskey," Catherine said.

"I'll arrange it," Thayer said, and departed.

The bartender personally brought Catherine's whiskey and another glass of beer for Colin.

"Sound on the goose?" Catherine asked him.

"For heaven's sake, shut up," Colin said to her.

"As a matter of fact, madam, I am not," said the bartender, in an unmistakable Boston accent. "But, as nearly everyone else here *is*, you should be careful to whom you address that question."

"Why did he call me madam?" Catherine said when he was gone. "I thought my disguise was better than that."

"It's good," Colin said, "but it doesn't completely cover you up, somehow."

When Thayer returned to the piano, he narrated in his falsetto the story of how Mike Fink had trimmed the darky's heel. The piano provided special effects.

"That's enough of that," Catherine said. "You can stay here if you want, but I'm leaving."

Colin followed her to the door, through the boisterous crowd, which had so fixed its attention on Thayer's narrative that it seemed to vomit laughter in the middle of every line. Catherine made her way through the thick necks and the rough red shirts. So many open mouths, and so few teeth. Jittering, rough faces blocked the entrance. Catherine pushed them aside. Tears of rage appeared in her eyes.

When Colin joined her on the street, he saw that she was weeping. "There, there," he said.

"There, there, *nothing!*" Catherine shouted, sobbing. She picked up a stone and threw it at a window of the saloon, but it missed its mark and only struck the cedar shakes.

"My goodness," Colin said.

Now Catherine wept in a great bitter convulsion while Colin

held her in his arms. They walked toward a grove of black walnut. The moon illuminated the ruins of Lawrence, with its blackened cellar holes and isolated chimneys, its dead horses and disabled wagons, its intoxicated looters still prising cooking accessories from the scorched stones of fireplaces. Under the moon, prairie flowers that the New Englanders had transplanted and tamed still bloomed in the neat gardens: verbena, petunias, foxglove, phlox, larkspur, spiderwort.

"Nothing is as nice as I thought it was going to be," Catherine said. "I waited for you all those months, and every day I thought how wonderful it would be when you came home. I watched the angle of the sun rising, and saw how the days were getting longer; and the longer the days got, the more hopeful I was, because it meant you would be coming soon. I put crosses on a map to show where you were, from the postmarks on McKay's letters. I really didn't do anything the whole time you were gone but miss you.

"Once, as I was looking out of the window of the hotel, a whirlwind dipped down out of a black cloud. It seemed to wander this way and that across the prairie, and people said it was coming in our direction. It made a hissing and roaring noise, and its inside was bright with a continuous fire. I thought, It's come to take me away, and I went out of doors to meet it, but then it abruptly went back into the cloud, and ten minutes later the sun was shining. The Germans moaned how thankful they were to have been spared, but I had this peculiar feeling I had missed a boat or a train that would have taken me directly to you.

"I thought it would be so very nice when you came home, but first you tell me that unkind lie about proposing marriage to a woman with no legs, and then Eli Thayer shows up wearing a dress and telling those horrid Mike Fink stories. I hate Mike Fink stories. Every one of them is nothing but boasting, and savagery, and killing bears by squeezing them, and shooting jars out of people's hands. I know he only tells those stories to make himself popular with the border ruffians, but if you ask me, he overdoes it. He could just sit at the piano and play and sing quietly, and no one would know he was there. He doesn't have to make himself the center of attention. He does it because he wants to. He's a big show-off."

They walked together until they left the ruin of Lawrence behind, and climbed Mount Oread, following the tracks the iron howitzer tires had made in the soft ground the previous month. At the summit, they sat for several hours talking, until Catherine's melancholy lifted and disappeared. Across the river, smoke rose from the dwellings of the Kaw half-breeds. Nearer at hand were a few poor shanties of the Delaware. A male Indian wearing nothing but vermilion and ocher mixed with grease sprang out of one of the shanties at regular intervals crying, "Ha, ha, ha," and shot arrows into the air. His children, also naked, fetched them back for him.

"Anyway, nothing is likely to come of it," Colin said.

"Why?"

"Because she's not as enthusiastic as I am."

There was a pause. Catherine looked into the valley, where a fog was now accumulating.

"How could any one not be enthusiastic about you?"

He took her hand and held it to his cheek. "I don't know," he said. "It's disappointing. I haven't found many women I wanted to marry."

"Well, what's in the way of it? Has she got another suitor? Does her mother want to keep her at home?"

"She doesn't have another suitor and she doesn't have a mother. If you asked her, she'd probably say she doesn't need these things, and she doesn't need me. She's made a strong habit of relying on herself."

163

A cold breeze rose up to them from the valley. "She may not *need* you," Catherine said, "but it might be nice to *have* you, even so."

"I don't think she puts it to herself that way," Colin said.

When they returned to the Thayers' later that night, they surprised Eli Thayer admiring his new hat in the hall mirror. The stovepipe looked quite ridiculous on his head, as he had not yet removed his dance-hall costume.

22

"Let's stop at Fish's," Catherine said, shortly after they left Lawrence, and it was agreed.

Mr. Paschal Fish, a Crow Indian, was the proprietor of a commercial establishment nine miles from Lawrence. On the lower floor was a dining room and a store of groceries and dry goods. On the upper floor were rooms Mr. Fish rented as sleeping apartments. Mr. Fish operated his establishment for the benefit of both red and white men. He was a dedicated admirer of the United States, particularly the phrase from her Declaration of Independence, "all men are created equal." He enthusiastically believed in education, and owned many books.

Colin and Catherine entered Mr. Fish's dining room and ordered luncheon, which turned out to be a choice of pigeon or catfish served with a blood porridge and corn bread. Mr. Fish himself brought them their food. His dogs followed him back and forth between the kitchen and the dining room. These dogs were large and dirty, but Mr. Fish himself was small and clean. His silver hair was gathered in a braid at the back of his head, and his blue eyes seriously regarded every question or comment put to him. Around Mr. Fish's neck hung a brass medal bearing the image and superscription of Queen Victoria.

The walls of the dining room were hung with a great number and variety of daguerreotypes. Most of these were ninth plates, a standard two inches by two and a half, but there were also several quarter plates and one large whole plate in an oval frame nearly ten inches in length. Each picture resided in its own wooden case, with the image protected by glass. Reflections of the light coming through the windows made it necessary to avoid certain angles when viewing the images. The cheeks of the people represented in the portraits were silver-blue, and their eyes were absolutely black.

A prevailing theme of the pictures was the local landscape, its trees, animals, and people. Dignified Shawnee elders wearing capes of pigeon wings and necklaces of bear claws stared into the dining room, their expressions giving no evidence of approval or disapproval of the whites in their midst spitting out catfish bones. A sequence of portraits showed a very old Indian, perhaps Fish's father, at work on his shanty, skinning a squirrel, eating at a table of women, sleeping with his dogs surrounding him on his bed. In the picture showing him eating with the women, he sat at one end of the table and they at the other, a variety of bowls and vessels separating them. A dog at his feet had blurred himself by moving during the exposure.

The landscapes showed Crow tent villages, stands of hardwood trees bordering curved brooks, and prairie. All of this seemed absolutely undisturbed by the daguerreotypist, perhaps

166

even uncomposed by him. And there were several pictures of the same Negro, in different positions and costumes, generally wearing the same ornaments the Indians had worn in the other pictures.

"Who is that?" Catherine asked Mr. Fish.

He returned in a moment with the actual Negro. This was Prince Bee, the cook in Mr. Fish's establishment and his partner in the daguerrean art. Mr. Fish explained how the two of them had made all the daguerreotypes in the room. An itinerant daguerreotypist had left his equipment in settlement of a debt. They had taught themselves the elaborate sensitization and development process, and were now capable of producing likenesses of excellent quality.

Prince Bee was a runaway slave. From the time of his escape, he had lived in the swamp with other runaways, stealing pigs and cattle from the plantations to keep alive. Life in the swamp had been very bad. He had lived in as much danger from the other runaways as from the snakes and the slave catchers. In some years there was cannibalism. Children were born in the swamp, and lived and died there as wild people. There was very little light, and no solid ground. It was a peculiar kind of freedom, without any pleasure or comfort.

But even this freedom ended eventually for Prince Bee. He had robbed the cowbell from a Sioux burial platform and hung it around his own neck. The Sioux included these bells with the effects of their dead to keep the carrion eaters away. Prince Bee had seen how the crows and vultures were frightened when they landed on the burial platform and shook the bells. Considering his own death, he stole one of the bells and suspended it from his neck, so that his eyes would not become bird food on the same day they closed for the last time. He had happened upon the bodies of black men in the swamp often enough to have legitimate fears of this kind. But with the bell around his neck, the Sioux tracked him and captured him easily, and sold him again into slavery, this time within the Sioux nation. He suffered terribly among the Sioux, as his years in the swamp had infected his feet with a curious brown plant which grew under the skin. Eventually Paschal Fish had bought his freedom in exchange for a pair of silk stockings. Now he had recovered his health, and seemed pleased.

A part of his pleasure was based on his new life with Mr. Fish in Kansas, and a part was based on forgetfulness. He had seen the white overseers take the bottom rail out of a fence and stick the black man's head in the hole, and let the weight of the rails down on his neck, and beat him until he was dead. He had seen two Negroes forced to copulate in a corncrib for the entertainment of whites. He had been married, and his wife and children had been taken away and sold, and so he depended on forgetfulness every day the way a physician depends on his memory.

From Paschal Fish's store, Catherine and Colin traveled directly to their own settlement. It was late afternoon when they stopped on the rise overlooking their valley. The western margins of the hotel and the superstructure of the *Princess* were framed in the same red light. The steamboat now sat on dry ground, heeled severely to starboard.

"My God," said Colin. "Is that a hole in it, under the paddle wheel?"

"No," Catherine told him. "It's only a shadow."

They found Gordon McKay sitting on the front porch of the hotel. He appeared to be in considerable difficulty. Tears came to his eyes for no particular reason. His voice cracked as he asked someone for the time of day. There was every reason for legitimate anxiety—it was reported that there were five men hanging from trees between Lawrence and Westport—but McKay's anxiety could not be attached to anything this specific. There was something crushing him, a sense of disappointment and loss, but he had no identifiable loss to blame.

Each day he watched the new bees, and asked Sewall after their health. He feared constantly for their magnificent energy.

In the next week, McKay attempted to bring some sense of organization back into his affairs, but no one who is himself bewildered can provide cogent direction for other people. He lay on his bed and listened to the sound of axes as Colin and Sewall continued the construction of the dam and its locks. There was now some urgency in this construction, because it grew plainer each day, as the border ruffians hung Northern people on the lovely old cottonwood trees, that the *Princess* might be needed for purposes of escape instead of the commercial purposes originally intended for her. If the river could be raised and the *Princess* floated, it might be possible to steam away, taking along the largest part of the original investment. Listening to the sounds of this activity, McKay felt a morbid shame. He occasionally sat up and searched under his bed for his boots, intending to go out and help, but more often he visited the kitchen and fed himself instead. He made glorious plates of fruit and sweets, and ate them sitting in one of the chairs on the front porch. As he ate quantities of strawberries and cream, he spoke to himself in harsh terms. I must not allow myself to get any fatter. I must send off my dues to the Athenaeum in case it becomes necessary to return to Boston. I must think of what to do.

But the bees came into his thoughts more often than any other consideration.

They are, of course, venomous, like snakes. He had noticed that when one bee stung, the others worked themselves into a frenzy and often stung near the same place. He recalled Jiffy's suffering when the hive came apart in the river. The bees had flown at him and attacked him, and he had been helpless. If bees could be made tame, like dogs, it might be possible to call them off such a senseless attack. One could shout at them, and rebuke them, and shame them, and send them back into their hives. But bees are never tame, even when they live in movable-frame hive boxes and work in the service of a beekeeper. Even then, they are perfectly wild. If a swarm issues from a beekeeper's hive, it goes directly to a hollow tree, and happily makes its home there. Similarly, an itinerant swarm may be captured and put to work in a Langstroth hive with no period of transition, no taming. This is apparently proof that bees in the wild and bees kept for agricultural purposes are no different.

But he also knew, from reading beekeepers' publications, that bees may be manipulated in the most extraordinary ways without harm. He knew, for example, that some beekeepers grew bee beards. This was done by placing the queen on one's chin. The bees would cluster around her, layer upon layer, until one was supporting a mass of thousands of bees on one's chin and throat. This great cone, soft and heavy, could ultimately hang down below the waist. In the absence of any threat, the bees would remain calm.

McKay was reminded, as he thought of bee beards, of the age of beekeepers. Langstroth was an old man; Dzierzon was older still. Beekeepers are generally old men, white and sterile. The bees themselves are old women, women without children, past softness. They are each other's captives, partners in a marriage where there are no smiles, no kisses, no words even, only slavery and stinging.

And these are terrible tortures, slavery and stinging! In a beautiful landscape, among flowers and calm rural prospects, the beekeeper and his bees struggle with one another in loveless arrangements. Every day, the bees fly thousands of miles in his service, and each one makes a drop of honey. He is their master, the owner of their product from the moment it is created. But there is no stability in this arrangement, because it is unnatural. They may decide in an instant to swarm away, or kill him with their stings, or both.

One morning as he was putting on his clothes, McKay felt a shade pulled tightly around his head, and knew at once that he was under the spell of the same depressive madness which afflicted Langstroth. The disease, he understood in this moment, was a disease of the bees, which they somehow transmitted to their keeper. He sat on his bed and braced himself with his arms. He did this because the walls were lurching without warning. His trousers lay in a heap around his ankles. His legs extended into them like wooden pilings into mud. Langstroth's terrible disease, which could turn a man's brain to wax!

There was no rhythm now to his breathing—it came at odd moments in puffs. What was the mechanism of this disease, which suffocated a man's pleasure? He visualized the passages of the brain inhabited by microscopic bees, building their comb. They trailed their stings behind them, turning the gray matter aside the way a plow turns the earth. They went about this destruction with their usual melancholy.

But he must fight them! He must not lie in bed as Langstroth had done, and let the infection become consolidated around his spirit. He pulled up his trousers, and marched downstairs, and announced that he meant to kill the bees with brimstone. He said this to a three-year-old German girl, the daughter of one of the clockmakers. She did not know what he was talking about. There happened to be no one else present on the first floor of the hotel.

He went into the workshops and searched until he found the torches and brimstone. The brimstone was yellow and heavy. Its surface was as uneven and pockmarked as an owl's cough-ball. McKay absently touched his hand to his face and was apalled to find that he hadn't yet shaved today. He considered whether he should shave first or kill the bees first. There was no clear reason why one should be done before the other.

171

He came out of the workshop, and slowly, slowly rounded the corner of the building until he had a view of the hives. Sewall had set them on the southern slope of a rise, close behind the hotel. The bees flew in and out, or waited their turn in the air to use the entrance. They suspected nothing.

He considered how he would murder them. He would set the brimstone fire on the west, and allow the wind to carry the fumes into the hives. Inside, the bees would roar with their wings and rush for the entrance, but they would be trapped. They would sting the combs and the hive box and each other in their confusion. They would die in a mad convulsion of anger and energy.

But now tears came into McKay's eyes and he wept loudly. He could not destroy the bees. He dropped the brimstone and covered his eyes and wept and wept.

In the note he left for Colin and Catherine, he explained how a vision of mercy had come to him, a vision which had commanded him to spare the lives of the bees. He was returning to Boston, the note said, to keep the bees safe from harm. He had opened the drawers of Catherine's desk where she kept the accounts and had taken a great deal of money.

23

A WEEK after McKay's departure, Paschal Fish and Prince Bee arrived in the daguerreotypist's wagon. This was a grand red Conestoga with a wooden roof which had been made in Lockport, New York, especially for the daguerreotypist, on the occasion of the beginning of his westward journey. It was pulled by oxen, and built with heavy oak beams and plates. An elaborate filigree outlined the margins of the roof. The roof itself was shingled in slate. Large black letters on the side, framed in gold, said,

CHARLES D. ELFELT
SKYLIGHT DAGUERREAN GALLERY

Prince Bee's head projected through the open skylight as they approached. As his head moved, it looked like a black bug running up and down the slates. This was apparently his habit, to ride this way, standing on a chair inside the wagon. He surveyed the prairie ahead and behind with a serene expression, and steadied himself with his elbows against the roof. His lids drooped. Only half of the sights of the prairie reached his eyes; half of its beauty, half of its danger. On the horizon, he might have been able to see smoke from the fires of slave catchers' camps; he might have seen black men hanging from trees; he might have caught sight of his wife and children standing on a high platform—but he looked up to the horizon so infrequently that he missed all this. He looked down instead, and watched the heavy spokes turning, each one sliding down to take the whole weight in its turn, partners in a strict agreement.

In the cypress swamp, where the water and the things which grew in it dissolved his feet from morning until dark, he had imagined himself riding above the earth at a height of ten feet, as he was now. With no effort, he could move, in his mind, from one end of the swamp to the other, and feel the motion as a breeze on his face. At this height, the slave catchers' dogs might come splashing through the vines, and sniff directly under him, and never catch his scent.

He listened for the bells on their collars, but heard instead Bernadette talking and laughing.

She sat beside Mr. Fish on the driver's bench. She was telling him something private and amusing. At the end of her story, the Indian also laughed, with a curious rising and falling tone in his voice, a sound almost purposely like the warbling of a bird.

They stopped the oxen in front of the hotel. There seemed to be no human beings about, but a goose warned them off. Mr. Fish lifted Bernadette down from the driver's bench and seated her on the front steps. He wanted to make a daguerreotype of her. Prince Bee brought the camera, with its brass-

174

mounted lens and its ground-glass screen. He also brought out the iodizing box and its wooden cup for the particles of iodine, the mercury bath, the box of silvered plates, and the alcohol lamp. The camera, a rosewood Scovills No. 2, had been manufactured in Waterbury, Connecticut, by J. M. L. and W. H. Scovill in the previous year.

The first task in the operation, that of buffing the plate, fell to Prince Bee. He began by turning over the edges of the copper and silver plate with a plate bender. This allowed the plate to be gripped by the plate block, which in turn was firmly fixed in the plate vise. He sprinkled the plate with rottenstone. Then, making slow parallel strokes with the buff stick, he cleaned the surface until it was even and smooth. Now he took up a second buff stick, this one covered with silk, and applied a dust of jeweler's rouge. Again he polished the surface, with an energy which threatened to wear away the silver coating entirely. When the buffing was finished, the plate appeared black.

Prince Bee now passed the plate into a tent, where Mr. Fish received it. The plate was then put into a coating box containing iodine crystals, and changed color immediately. It became yellow, then orange and red, then yellow again. Next it went into the second coating box, where the quickstuff changed its color to a pale rose. Finally it went back into the iodine for a few moments, and then into the plate shield, where it would be protected from light until it went in the camera. Mr. Fish was coughing and retching as he came out of the tent. The ugly smell of iodine and bromine compounds followed him the way farts follow a sick person.

The camera was now erected in front of Bernadette on its elegant tripod. Prince Bee carried the heavy iron head-vise out of the wagon and adjusted it to accommodate the back of Bernadette's head. He instructed her to keep her weight firmly against it. Mr. Fish went under the black cloth and studied his composition on the ground-glass screen. Bernadette's face hovered behind the glass, white and fair and highlighted at its margins by a rainbow of chromatic aberration. A man appeared in the picture.

"Oh, Colin," Bernadette said. "I *am* glad to see you, but could you please stand off a little bit and let Mr. Fish finish? He's doing my portrait."

The exposure required twenty-five seconds. When it was completed, the plate was placed over the vapors of the mercury bath, a pyramidal cast-iron pot supported on an iron stand over the alcohol lamp. Mr. Fish held the plate in the vapors for exactly two minutes by his pocket watch. Next he held the plate, with a pair of pliers, directly over the alcohol lamp, and poured over its surface a solution of hyposulphite of soda to remove the unexposed coating of silver halide. Now came a solution of gold chloride and sodium thiosulphate. Finally he rinsed the plate in water, and dried it over the alcohol lamp.

Prince Bee brought a leather case out of the wagon, and together they mounted the daguerreotype inside it, behind a thin sheet of glass. When it was finished, Mr. Fish brought it to Bernadette and put it in her hands.

She studied it for several minutes before speaking.

"I love it," she said. "I *love* daguerreotypes. I saw my first one in Pittsburgh, just before coming here, and it was so beautiful I felt I could weep. I felt its power, and yet I wondered, Why is it so powerful? It has no colors; it is all done in simple chiaro-oscuro, and I had always felt before that the persuasion of a painting or a drawing was at least as much in its colors as its shapes. But then I took up a lens and put it over the image. I moved the lens to a place where a shop sign was just barely visible in the distance, and the lens magnified the image twenty times, so that the letters all stood out clearly. I looked at the individual bricks in a hundred city buildings, and I could see each one in precise detail, even the chips in the individual bricks. The most skillful miniaturist with the finest brush might have produced the same effect the daguerreotype gives to the naked eye, but he could never, you see, *never* produce the accuracy that the lens can see. The lens shows that the *thing itself* is frozen in the daguerreotype. No one has ever made a picture like this before."

Bernadette's baby, which had been sleeping in the wagon, woke up and began to cry. Mr. Fish brought it to her solemnly. She took the Indian by the hand before he could escape, and drew him down to her and kissed him on the mouth. "Thank you," she said. "I'll keep it with me all my life."

Catherine now joined them on the porch, and watched as Mr. Fish and Prince Bee poured the chemicals back into glass bottles and returned the equipment to the wagon. They brought out Bernadette's chair, and her trunk. Before they departed, Prince Bee took up his position at the skylight. They drove away without looking back.

"Did you see those big shotguns he had under his seat?" Catherine asked. "I wonder what he does with them."

"He kills people with them," Bernadette told her.

This was the truth. The two horses which were tied to the tailgate of Fish's wagon had been the property of two gentlemen from Missouri earlier that morning. These gentlemen had stopped the wagon in a lonely spot on the prairie and attempted to seize Prince Bee. Mr. Fish had blown them up, two barrels apiece, so that bits of their bodies flew everywhere, and their blood fell like rain into the tall grass. When they had buried the men and tied their horses to the wagon, Mr. Fish and Prince Bee had brought out a luncheon of prairie dove and watercress, which they had shared with Bernadette before driving on.

In the next week, the Crow kept saying that terrible armies were riding across Kansas in all directions. This news alarmed everyone, particularly Edward and Jiffy. They wanted to go home to their parents because of the coming war, but were afraid to travel alone for fear of being impressed into one army or another. They had not heard from their parents for eight months, and felt the lack of information acutely. In her youth, their mother had been interested in astronomy and had built several telescopes. She had taught her children to recognize old friends in the constellations. Now, as the armies obstructed passage along the riverbanks, Edward and Jiffy considered striking out for home over land, with the stars to guide them. But they had no maps, and in fact had very little idea what natural features of the land might lie between Kansas and Mississippi. They might encounter bad weather, and be unable to consult the sky for directions. They might come to unknown mountains or inland seas. They might drown in a swamp, and be eaten by the reptiles and birds.

They missed their mother's affection, and they missed her common sense, but they also missed her beauty, which was still considerable, even after forty-five years of poverty. They wondered whether they would ever see her again.

Colin lay beside Bernadette in bed, considering how strange it was to be happy in the midst of mortal dread. His hand, resting on her sternum, rose and fell, and therefore waved goodbye. Goodbye to what?

Goodbye, perhaps, to an entire episode of seeking, which was now definitely at an end. The travel on the *Princess* to the new lands, the exploration of the prairie, the journey to New England were all parts of this same seeking, which sometimes seemed to take him, in the company of other people, toward a place, and other times toward a person, but never to a satisfactory consummation, never to a discovery. What is it that sustains the energy of the young person who peers into disused icehouses, who stops to read the names of the inhabitants of apartment buildings, who attends the birthday parties of distant cousins? This person is seeking something, but will not be able to tell you what it is. He must remain alert for it, and yet he is not certain he will recognize it when it appears. It will be an opportunity, like the opportunity to buy and sell a piece of real estate for quick profit, or meet an easy woman, and take her home, and spread her legs.

But these are transient opportunities, and one is prepared to believe that there are also longer-lasting ones.

Kansas, of course, represented a very rich opportunity. Settlers arriving from the East were invariably surprised that it had not been discovered and farmed before now. Colin was reminded of the harvest celebration at the end of the previous summer. Edward and Jiffy had only planted a tiny patch of soil in vegetables, but the produce had overwhelmed them. Game practically walked in the door and hopped in the pot. The bees had prospered. When the final harvest had been completed, the bees had produced a surplus of more than five hundred pounds of honey and one hundred pounds of wax all in their first year. McKay had said that the black soil would be one part food and the rest money, and he had been right.

Colin recalled the preparations for the celebration. Catherine had fired a great collection of plates and gravy dishes for the purpose, since the Crow's affection for gravy was well known. Catherine's kiln had been kept white-hot for a day, shooting flames up its chimney with the energy of thousands of continuous Chinese rockets. The Crow children had stood in front of the kiln and stretched out their fingers, catching the heat. He had supervised the kiln from the distance of the hotel porch, where he worked with the German ladies on the silk balloon.

It had required so many thousands of stitches, and he had worked on it for such a length of time, that even now, a year later, he still had a vivid impression of pushing the needle

179

through the folds of silk. As the panels were assembled, the spherical shape grew plainer. This had been a small balloon, but there was no reason why its proportions should not be doubled or tripled. . . .

"Wake up," Colin said. "I've just had a thought."

"I don't want to wake up," Bernadette said.

"You will when you hear this. We're going to escape in a giant balloon."

In his mind, the balloon he saw now was of such vast proportions that the entire company, from the Germans to Edward and Jiffy, could be accommodated in its car. Even Langstroth's bees would not be left behind. Its dome of silk would stand as tall as the hotel, and its great volume would hold the heat for days instead of hours. They would leave the invading army behind to stare at their shadow as it crossed the clouds. A firebox suspended below the bag would add extra heat, and this would appear as a red eye from the earth . . .

"It doesn't sound practical," Bernadette said.

The Germans, who had ignored the politics of Kansas until the present moment, were now quite numb with fear and worry. Should they wear traditional dress and speak their native language, to avoid being taken for Yankees? Should they address a petition for their safety to the Missouri Militia? Or would it be safer to buy red shirts and dirty mules, and escape by impersonating the border rascals themselves? They considered and rejected all of these possibilities as their panic deepened.

One morning they were simply gone, and no one knew where they went. They might have gone east or they might have gone west, and as they had not asked directions or left a note, it was impossible to say. It was presumed, on the evidence that they had taken their Old Dog Tray music boxes

180

with them, that they were headed for Missouri.

Bernadette rolled herself into the carpenters' shops on the day they left. Under ordinary circumstances, it would be impossible to speak in normal tones in this room and be heard. Now the room was silent, and even the finest dust had fallen out of the air. It made the benches seem long abandoned. Parallel tracks stretched out behind her wheels, and stopped underneath her like the unfinished Western Railway. Piled against one of the walls, she found what she had come to find, the stockpile of unassembled hive bodies. Here were the sides and there were the ends, each one mortised to fit the other. From these materials, McKay had planned to build a giant apiary.

"Well, they're back," Colin said as he came into the shop. "The Germans. They're all in the kitchen, feeding themselves to get over their fright. They ran into a whole army three miles from here." He laid a lady's-slipper in Bernadette's lap.

"This is nice," she said. "Where did you find it?"

"In the woods, near the place where Sewall is digging his beetles."

"I like it."

"I thought you would," Colin said.

"I suppose the Germans are all upset?"

"Yes," he said, "they are. It's almost worth worrying about, having a horde of border ruffians headed this way."

"Do I remember your saying that those people were afraid of bees? The border people?" Bernadette asked.

"What do you have in mind?"

"I thought we might arrange ourselves in the middle of an apiary," she said. "Here are all the parts."

Colin surveyed the stacks of cut-out boxes. They reached the ceiling. There must have been materials for a thousand hives. He looked at Bernadette and was powerfully drawn to her. "That doesn't sound practical," he said, bending to kiss her. "But let's do it anyway, because it's your idea, and you're so very, very dear."

At this moment, William Sewall was walking through range grass. The grass was waist-high in places, making the going slow. His target was a flag sticking up above the stems and leaves, which he had improvised some days earlier by tying a handkerchief to a long stick.

Beneath the flag was the corpse of a squirrel he had left here as bait. He had developed an enthusiasm for the family *Silphidae,* the carrion beetles, and had left this squirrel as his agent to collect specimens. The members of this family are mostly medium or large size, some species attaining a length of nearly two inches. These beetles usually feed upon decaying animal matter, although some species will eat fungi, and a few will even destroy and eat members of their own species.

He probed the squirrel with his knife, and was well rewarded. It was infested with burying beetles, of the genus *Necrophorus.* The body of this genus is very stout, almost cylindrical, and the antennae are enlarged to form a compact club. They are burying beetles because they bury carrion, removing the earth beneath it to allow it to settle into the ground. When it has descended below the surface of the earth, they cover it again, and at last the female tunnels down to it and lays her eggs within it. The larvae thus come to life in a rich grave. In the course of watching these beetles, Sewall had often been impressed by their great strength. He had once seen a pair of them roll a dead rat several feet to a soft plot of ground, where they buried it in ten minutes.

From the same carcass, he also collected some rove beetles, the *Staphylinidae.* These are swift and nasty animals, and will lift their abdomens, as if threatening to sting, when disturbed. Being beetles, they cannot sting, of course, but their resemblance to some of the larger species of wasps makes this gesture believable to many of their attackers. Sewall only smiled at them and scooped them up.

Throughout the afternoon, he walked the perimeter of one of his ever-larger circles. These circles, centering on the hotel, were precisely measured beetle domains. Within them, he catalogued the species and marked down the details of terrain preferred by each. He had, earlier this morning, encountered an army from Missouri camped on one of his most productive field sites. Unknown to Sewall, this army was led by Bucky Dragon, now a colonel in the Missouri Militia. The discovery had annoyed him considerably, since it required him to do without evidence which could have an important bearing on his conclusions.

He had made up his mind to get the information which would allow him to estimate the number of beetle species in Kansas, and had developed very careful procedures for the purpose. The presence of Dragon's army cut a notch into one of his circles, introducing an error he did not know how to correct.

When the evidence was complete, he would take the earliest passage to England and confront Darwin with it. There was a point in Darwin's manuscript where he discussed the topographical constraints upon the propagation of species, and cited instances in the fossil record which showed how parallel evolution had depended upon the presence of natural barriers. It was here that Sewall knew that he had Darwin by the balls, since the plains of Kansas have no natural barriers, and yet he, Sewall, had found isolated pockets of beetle species entirely unlike others only a half-mile away. He would put this information down before Darwin plainly and truthfully.

But what would Darwin do with it? He might ignore it. He might refuse to believe it, coming, as it did, from an amateur, someone without a university degree. This was such a threatening possibility that Sewall considered he might have to represent himself as a college man in order to get an audience. And yet, any falsification, even this unimportant one, would be an unhappy way to begin a scientific collaboration.

In the evening, he stood on the rise overlooking the hotel and the river. The sun had descended only moments ago. The sky was a yellow color which would mean rain. There were lights at every window in the hotel, but the whole population was apparently in the workshops, where singing and the pounding of hammers could be heard through open doors and brilliant windows. They were all at work, even a party of Crow whose ponies stood outside the door, but what were they doing? The Germans had long ago taught the Indians drinking songs, and now the Crow could not drink a glass of beer without singing.

Sewall maintained a buried cache of his records and specimens, and now he dug this up. The thought crossed his mind that the results of his research might lie in this box after his death and never come to light. Dying, of course, is not at all terrible unless one is certain to be forgotten. The apprehension that beetles from the outside would be the only discoverers of the beetles on the inside of his box filled Sewall with a sharp fear.

24

"I WISH they'd be quiet," Catherine said, speaking of the Crow. "How many times can one bear listening to 'Ein Feste Burg Ist Unser Gott' sung in a beery falsetto? Someone should tell them to go home. They'll wake the baby."

"They're our friends," Colin said. "They want to stand by us. We can't tell them to go home just because they're singing."

"Listen to that," Catherine said. "There's the baby crying. I told you so."

"Bring him here," Bernadette said. "I'll feed him."

"It's no trouble for me to feed him," Catherine said. "I have some corn cake I could give him."

"He gets milk in the morning," Bernadette explained. "I need to feed him. I'm leaking."

They were sitting in the wicker chairs on the front porch.

This was just before dawn. Colors were beginning to come back to things. The white bear claws in the Crow's cloaks. The alarming, tilted shape of the *Princess* on the dark river flats. The horizon and its mountains were almost distinct. Animals were moving among the hives, stopping to sniff at the entrance of each one—these were the dogs of the Crow.

The sun was rising. Shadows from an aspen twenty feet away stood sharply on the wall of the hotel. Where the shadow reached across a window, it seemed to have broken the glass.

"I think I see somebody," Bernadette said.

"Where?"

"On the other side of that cottonwood, by the river. A man on a mule."

"I don't see anything," Colin said.

"He's gone now."

"It was a scout," Sewall told them. "There's a whole army on the other side of that hill."

Colin went into the hotel to rouse the Germans. They were resting in their rooms, wearing all their clothes. They put on their bee veils and gloves, and rushed out into the yard.

Now it was possible to hear the army approaching. Its dogs warned the dogs of the Crow. The dogs of the Crow answered back, using filthy language. The Crow themselves had disappeared.

When the army came forward from the cottonwood trees, it was apparent that the Missourians were drunk, even at this early hour. Their mules were laden not only with men, but with heavy objects. One man carried a glass chandelier behind his saddle; another had a carved and upholstered armchair. Their hounds snarled and crouched at the mules' feet. Their chief preceded them. This was Bucky Dragon. His horse staggered under the weight of a grandfather clock.

But now the army had seen the apiary, and had drawn up short. Close to a thousand hives were arranged around the hotel, and the Germans stood among them wearing veils and gloves, apparently ready to upset the hives and release billions of angry bees. The part of the army which had halted was jostled by the part coming up from behind.

Catherine returned from the kitchen. Something she had seen among the depraved faces, among the caried teeth and tallowed whiskers, among the rough red shirts and bad-smelling pants, had made her break into heavy sobs. Colin looked at her for an explanation. She brought his attention to the man who was wearing Eli Thayer's stovepipe hat.

"They're all dead," she said.

She stepped off the porch and approached Dragon's horse. The low sun made a shadow stand out ahead of her. She held an iron cooking pan by her side, concealed among the folds of her skirt. Dragon squinted into the glare, shading his eyes with his hand. Catherine approached him step by step. Her hair was brilliant with reflections: white lights and colors.

"Which one of you killed that baby?" she said.

Dragon moved his head this way and that, apparently trying to make her out against the sun.

The Missourians' mules had come equipped with their own flies. Something about the morning light pointed each one out, demonstrating its track up and down among the swishing tails.

"Did you kill the baby for his cuckoo clock?"

Catherine addressed this question to Dragon, but Dragon apparently still couldn't see her properly. Overhead, honey-bees flew in from distant fields. They looked like shooting stars.

Catherine raised the iron pan over her head and swung it down, striking Dragon and his horse a glancing blow. The horse reared, spilling the clock on the ground with a terrible crash. "You killed a nice little baby for his cuckoo clock!" She continued swinging the pan, battering men and mules in all directions. Horse chopping! People chopping! The bees watched all this from a substantial altitude, and went about their busi-

187

ness. Catherine was knocked down and lost from sight.

Seeing this, Colin approached the tangle of animals at a dead run. Dust rising from so many hoofs obscured the ground. The army was moving in every direction at once. He found Catherine crouched in the dirt, weeping and rocking back and forth. The shadows of horses and riders passed over her, but these were their shadows only and not their hoofs.

When he attempted to pick her up, she kicked him. When he attempted it again, she kicked him again.

He stood back. It was clear enough that the kicks had been deliberate, and would continue to be. He walked around her, but she pivoted as he did, keeping her feet coiled under her. Her eyes threatened—Leave me alone, I'll kill you, too!—but she said nothing.

He wondered whether she still had her weapon, and then he saw it lying some distance away. The last of the whirling animals disappeared, and the sun struck his back again. He squatted beside Catherine and spoke softly into her ear. "What's all this kicking?"

"I'm scared," she whispered.

"What?"

"I'm scared," she said. "I'm so scared."

Eventually she let him pick her up. Her back was arched, its muscles rigid. The air was becoming still again, dropping dust back into the clay.

"I'm scared," Catherine said. The muscles of her back were hardened in a convulsion. "I'm scared, I'm scared."

They were alone. There on the porch were Bernadette, Sewall, Edward, and Jiffy, waiting. The Germans stood by their hives. The sun was rising, and in two hours more it would make a wind, and then it would make clouds from the wind, and then rain from the clouds. But for the moment, the air was quiet and blue.

"What are you scared of?" Colin whispered into his sister's ear. "They've gone."

25

"I DIDN'T KNOW he could actually *do* anything," Catherine said, speaking of McKay. "In Boston, he was full of talk, and nothing ever came of it. But here he actually *did* something. He built the hotel, and he almost made a success of the bees." She said all of this in the course of explaining why she had made up her mind to go with Sewall and the Germans back to Boston. "I'm really convinced that if things had been only slightly different, he might have made money from his bees. But, of course, you must believe this too, because you're staying."

Catherine packed her trunk. She rushed around the hotel scooping up her belongings. While she was doing this, she whistled Stephen Foster songs. She whistled "The Old Folks at Home" and "Massa's in the Cold, Cold Ground." As it was not generally known that Catherine could whistle, this caused some astonishment. Everyone agreed that Stephen Foster songs sounded better whistled than sung. Even Foster himself knew this, but he did not know the reason. He presumed that it had to do with the well-known whistling ability of darkies. With the exception of a trip to New Orleans in 1852, Foster himself had never been to the South, and therefore knew very little about darkies. He lived in Pittsburgh. Here he wrote "Louisiana Belle," "O Susannah," "Uncle Ned," "Away Down South," and all those other favorites which were later collected in *Songs of the Sable Harmonists.*

While Sewall and the Germans were loading her trunk on the wagon, Catherine had one more try at telling Colin and Bernadette her feelings concerning McKay.

"I suppose I would stay here with you if I thought I was so much better than him. But I'm not better than him. We're fairly well matched. Everyone has always said so."

Catherine tied a bonnet on her head as she said this.

"I'm certainly willing to admit that his running away was cowardly," she said. "And this whole plan, from buying the steamboat to establishing a town based on bees was absolutely reckless and outrageous. But he did it because he believed in a book, Langstroth's book. And that seems all right to me. The error of believing in a book seems to me a very human mistake."

While she was speaking, Sewall had come in and taken a recumbent position on a couch, one leg on a chair, to read a newspaper. This was his habit, to be frequently horizontal, on a couch, on the floor, on the grass, anywhere. By the time Catherine had finished speaking, he had put the newspaper down and was lost in thought, or perhaps only gloom. He looked into the distance. In the weeks since he had returned from Massachusetts, his friends considered that he had become a hopeless victim of melancholy and might soon stop all useful activity. His lids drooped, but the eyes beneath them were beautifully soft and tender, almost femininely expressive. This lazy man had failed again and again to make an American fortune, but he apparently still had ambition.

It was the ambition of a kitten. He was almost deliberately awkward as he undertook his adventures; he was playing, but there was no evidence that he was playing to win. Sewall loved kittens. One of his cats had just had a litter.

Jiffy asked him a question, and received absolutely no answer. Jiffy went out, leaving the door open. The Germans could be heard closing crates with their hammers. One of Sewall's cats could be seen through the open door, voiding in the tall grass. The animal bent its back into the form of a C, and its tail shuddered. Jiffy returned and sat in a chair. After more than thirty minutes, Sewall gave a perfectly reasonable answer to Jiffy's question. No one knew where his thoughts had been all that while, or why they could not be disturbed.

In the evening, Colin and Bernadette, now the only occupants of the hotel, retired to bed. As Colin latched the front door, he noted how the clock, still lying on the slope to the river, resembled a dead animal in the gathering darkness. He helped Bernadette remove her clothes and transfer herself from her chair onto the white sheets. He covered her with a down comforter and undressed himself.

"I felt badly sending Catherine off with such a case of nerves," Bernadette said. "She wasn't herself at all today. Not much of what she was telling us made any sense."

"She needs her own life."

"Is that what she was saying? Yes, perhaps it was. But I had the feeling she was leaving because she felt we were driving her away, and really it's the opposite."

How beautiful she looks there, Colin said to himself. Her hair is the color of oak leaves in winter, and her skin is as clear as ice. She is intelligent and high spirited. How could I be more fortunate?

"Do you know what she told me?" Bernadette said. "She

191

said she was going to make McKay buy a house for her, a particular house with blue walls and yellow shutters, and if she had such a house, she would be certain to have a baby. All this was revealed to her in a dream."

"Well, that *is* a little mad," Colin said, coming in beside her.

"I hope she does get her baby," Bernadette said.

Now she lay on the white sheets, and they supported her with a buoyancy like the buoyancy a body is given in water. None of us can fly; none of us is lighter than air. We are attached to the ground, and hold ourselves from it only with the greatest effort. Only in the water can we float, and there the crippled person is almost normal. He had seen Bernadette swimming in the river. They had gone together, in late summer, to a remote river beach, and taken off their clothes. Bernadette had crawled in, a beautiful crocodile. In the water, she dragged herself forward with powerful strokes.

And this pulling power was now partly his. They would be farmers, and they would also maintain the husbandry of the bees. There was no reason why they should not be prosperous. They were ready for the future.

Yet there was a question between them, a detail only, a trivial thing, but a question, certainly. It was this: Who was the father of Bernadette's child?

"I've only just this minute thought of Mr. Fish and Prince Bee," she said. "Their store is on the road between here and Lawrence."

He did not answer. He lifted the comforter and put his lips on her white skin.

"They must be safe," she said. "This is their country, after all. If they can't hide in it, no one can."

26

In 1859, the year that Darwin's *Origin of Species* appeared in print, Gordon McKay became interested in a machine invented by Lyman R. Blake which could sew the soles of shoes to the uppers, all in one operation. He acquired the patent from Blake, with the aid of investment by his mother. He hired the expert machinist R. H. Mathies to improve the machine and increase its speed. By 1862, the invention was working well enough to proceed into commercial production, and the McKay Association was formed to manufacture it. At this moment, the Civil War was creating a demand for army shoes, and within a short time, McKay had secured a federal contract for 25,000 pairs. In addition to producing shoes, he also offered the machine to other manufacturers on a royalty basis, and within one year was receiving more than half a million dollars from shoe and boot manufacturers from Maine to Ohio.

In this year, the worst one of the war, the President's son Willie died of a preventable disease, a simple fever which had been allowed to become pneumonia. Willie died on a Thursday, but was not buried until Monday. There was a heavy storm that weekend, and during this storm, the father did a strange thing. When the embalmer had finished his work, the father sent for Willie's favorite playmate, a boy by the name of Bud Bayne. The father greeted the youngster at the door, and took him through the quiet rooms to the nursery, where Willie had been placed in his bed. A chair was brought for Bud to the bedside. The father took down a storybook—it was Aesop's *Fables*—and began to read. Lincoln had been reading this book to the boys during Willie's illness. Although he read to them now as if Willie were still able to hear the words, as if the wistful expression the embalmer had fixed on Willie's face reflected the boy's appreciation of the cleverness of the crow who dropped the stones into the jug, there is no evidence that Lincoln was at this time, nor at any other time during the war, actually mad. The father is not deluded that his son is still alive. Instead, he seems to have willed himself into a dream, in which he has a sweet communion with the boys. But he has a sad consciousness that it is a dream only, and not reality.

At Willie's death, the war was already a year old. Bernadette's child had reached the age of seven, and now Colin and Bernadette were expecting a baby of their own. The armies of the South moved through Kansas, burning it and leaving it a desert behind them. All the plant matter in Kansas threatened to become the fuel for fires. The beetles exploded like popcorn. But Colin and Bernadette were safe, because they maintained the strength of the bees.

Gordon McKay and Catherine moved to Cambridge, where they occupied a pleasant house on Arrow Street. They became

194

the intimates of several Harvard faculty members. They particularly valued the friendship of the naturalist Louis Agassiz, a figure much beloved in Boston society. In these years, Agassiz was devoting all his energies to the public exposure of Darwin's fatuousness. Agassiz had shown, following Karl Ernst von Baer, that the life history of the individual repeats the life history of the type. Thus the changes which can be seen when animals move through embryonic growth coincide with the order of succession of the fossils through the geologic ages. But these changes should not be interpreted as evidence for Darwin. Agassiz demonstrated, using animal materials he carried around in a suitcase, that there need not be any genetic connection postulated between the Vertebrates, Articulates, Mollusks, and Radiates. They each need their own creation. But as he said this, his audiences, now aware of Darwin's contradictory evidence, remained uneasy.

It was an uneasiness which would finally upset the relationship between men and the animals forever. Later in that same year, when Lincoln freed the slaves, he made use of arguments which seemed to depend upon a revised scheme of creation. A divergence within the doctrines of natural history had suddenly imposed upon us all an unreasonable standard of fairness, and not a little guilt.

"What would you do in my position?" the President asked a Southern loyalist. "Would you drop the war where it is? Or would you prosecute it in the future with elder-stalk squirts charged with rose water?"

Stephen Foster wrote without rest, but it was clear that the public had little use for his music, which now seemed repetitious and commonplace. Something had changed. No one in the North had any idea what a Negro was, but they were beginning to suspect that E. P. Christy and his Minstrels were as vague on the subject as they were. *Foster's Ethiopian Melodies* and *Songs of the Sable Harmonists* quietly dropped out of print.

In his new songs, Foster tried to imagine how the Negroes' voices might be changed, now that they were free, but even he knew that there was no information on the subject. He drank a great deal. The Negroes' voices, once so mellow in his imagination, now fused into an angry buzzing. He fell into poverty and obscurity. In New York, he went from one music store to another, offering his songs for next to nothing. His health declined. He was admitted to Bellevue Hospital, where he lay near death in a charity ward.

In the midst of this epoch of disintegration, McKay's machinery stitched the uppers to the lowers. Thousands of boots came forward, and thousands of feet put them on and marched away. Having failed to establish beekeeping in Kansas, McKay, as much as any other man, was responsible for the prevention of Negro slavery there.

The McKay Association built machines to produce the machines, so that every month the number of shoe machines increased. In 1863, McKay lost track of their total number, and never knew it again. He only knew there were very, very many of them, and they were all working for him.

And what a great pleasure Catherine took in the house on Arrow Street! She had it painted a dignified pale blue, with yellow trim. Behind the house was a deep garden surrounded by a wall. When she gave parties in this garden, her guests stared into the webs of her apples, her pears, her flowering dogwoods the way one would stare into a Yule fire at Christmas. The children of an adjacent professor helped her maintain this garden. The professor's eldest daughter, herself quite beautiful, confided in Catherine and asked her advice in matters of love. Catherine was flattered to give it.

This same year, McKay read in a novel by a foreigner that it was possible for human beings to have sex with their mouths.

Throughout the winter, he returned to the book again and again, and troubled himself a great deal over whether people could actually do what the writer said they were doing. Eventually he let the matter drop from his mind.

In later years, he concentrated his attention on the production of the stouter grades of shoes and boots, and on improvements in metallic fastenings for shoes. McKay's boots were the favorites of the many Bills who tamed the West. Wild Bill, Buffalo Bill, California Bill, Apache Bill, and Rattlesnake Bill all preferred them, and thereby added to his fortune.

Toward the end of his life, McKay enjoyed the friendship of his neighbor on Arrow Street, Nathaniel Southgate Shaler, then professor of geology and dean of the Lawrence Scientific School. With the encouragement of Professors Shaler and Agassiz, he signed a trust instrument providing that after his death, his whole estate should come to Harvard.

Each year, Catherine made a variety of elaborate preserves from the fruits which ripened in her garden. Traditionally, some of the candied pears, some of the green tomato relish, some of the rose hip jelly would be set aside for a particular purpose. At Commencement, McKay brought these products of his garden to share with the undergraduate classes at their breakfast convocation. It was a duty he looked forward to all the year. He would rise before dawn and dress carefully. From his bedroom, he could see the apple blossoms in his garden beginning to shine. The first honeybees were beginning to arrive. The low sun lit them dramatically as they came down, apparently not even using their wings, like stones thrown from a distance. Wealth! Its attainment is such a paradox! The bees were after it, and came to McKay's garden expecting it. But none of them ever became rich, because a fortuitous accident is required for that; hard work is never sufficient. Bees are not eligible for much in the way of wealth, in spite of their

197

integrity. This was how McKay explained it to himself as he knotted his tie. There is something delightful in the future, but it is beyond common work.

He left his door just as the light became strong enough to carry him toward the gates of the Yard. The heavy houses of his neighbors lay side by side, darkened by each other's shadows. He heard the undergraduates singing in his imagination. Soon he would be among the classes, enjoying their gratitude, feeling at ease and lighthearted.

Praise for Thomas McMahon's novels

The pleasures of Thomas McMahon's prose are constant. . . . He invests his story with a touching anarchic glee. There's a whimsical Kurt Vonnegut feel to *Loving Little Egypt*, at once funny and sad and altogether engaging.

—*Newsday.*

Stimulating and bold . . . McMahon is out to explore the spirit, the mind, and the ethics and aesthetics of invention.   —*Los Angeles Times*